"What's got me curious is where they got their weapons."

The Executioner took the weapon from the lawman, quickly fieldstripped it and inspected its various parts. "I'd say it hasn't been fired before today," he observed. Looking up at Handler, he added, "You can't buy these in gun shops around here."

"Right. They're automatic, so they're illegal to own without a federal license. But where are they getting them?"

Bolan didn't know, no more than he knew how the Carolina Militia ambusher knew when he'd arrived. He had some hard questions to ask Hal Brognola.

It was obvious there was a leak at the top....

Other titles available in this series:

Stony Man Doctrine	Hellground
Terminal Velocity	Inferno
Resurrection Day	Ambush
Dirty War	Blood Strike
Flight 741	Killpoint
Dead Easy	Vendetta
Sudden Death	Stalk Line
Rogue Force	Omega Game
Tropic Heat	Shock Tactic
Fire in the Sky	Showdown
Anvil of Hell	Precision Kill
Flash Point	Jungle Law
Flesh and Blood	Dead Center
Moving Target	Tooth and Claw
Tightrope	Thermal Strike
Blowout	Day of the Vulture
Blood Fever	Flames of Wrath
Knockdown	High Aggression
Assault	Code of Bushido
Backlash	Terror Spin
Siege	Judgment in Stone
Blockade	Rage for Justice
Evil Kingdom	Rebels and Hostiles
Counterblow	Ultimate Game
Hardline	Blood Feud
Firepower	Renegade Force
Storm Burst	Retribution
Intercept	Initiation
Lethal Impact	Cloud of Death
Deadfall	Termination Point
Onslaught	Hellfire Strike
Battle Force	Code of Conflict
Rampage	Vengeance
Takedown	
Death's Head	

DON PENDLETON's
MACK BOLAN®

EXECUTIVE ACTION

A GOLD EAGLE BOOK FROM
WORLDWIDE®

TORONTO • NEW YORK • LONDON
AMSTERDAM • PARIS • SYDNEY • HAMBURG
STOCKHOLM • ATHENS • TOKYO • MILAN
MADRID • WARSAW • BUDAPEST • AUCKLAND

First edition January 2000

ISBN 0-373-61470-5

Special thanks and acknowledgment to
David North for his contribution to this work.

EXECUTIVE ACTION

Printed in U.S.A.

Whom men fear they hate,
and whom they hate they wish dead.

> —Quintus Ennius
> B.C. 239-169

Passionate hatred can give meaning and purpose to an empty life.

> —Eric Hoffer
> 1902-1983

Hate is a violent flame that can destroy even the strongest of nations if it is not promptly snuffed out.

> —Mack Bolan

CHAPTER ONE

"Please fasten your seat belts in preparation for takeoff."

Mack Bolan, aka the Executioner, heard the mechanical-sounding voice over the speaker system and opened his eyes. Fastening his seat belt, he glimpsed out his window. It was dusk and night was fast approaching.

Through the haze, he could see the outlines of Washington, D.C., begin to fade as the Boeing 727 began to accelerate down the runway.

Bolan was tired. The wounds from the last mission were still healing, and he'd gotten only a few hours of sleep before Hal Brognola, director of the Sensitive Operations Group, made contact with him.

Reluctantly, he had agreed to undertake a new mission.

This time he wouldn't be going up against the

Mafia, foreign agents or terrorists—unless an organized group that reacted violently to what they considered illegal interference in their lives by the federal government could be called terrorists.

The Carolina Militia.

The name echoed memories of the Revolutionary War and the civilian militia groups that fought the British for American liberty. According to Brognola, *this* militia was made up of a group of armed bigots who hated everyone different from them.

Their current target was a small group of Montagnards living at the edge of the Great Smoky Mountains Park on a farm commune. Hounded by the Vietnamese and other Southeast Asian Communist armies, the hill tribes, who had been America's closest allies in the Vietnam War, had been rescued from extinction years earlier by a grateful nation and given a new home in North Carolina.

Someone was waiting for Bolan in Asheville, a sheriff by the name of Doug Handler. According to Brognola, Handler could brief him on details of the situation.

The soldier leaned back in his seat. A flight attendant stopped in the aisle.

"Something to drink, sir?"

"Thanks, but I'd rather rest."

The young woman smiled and walked away.

As he closed his eyes to nap, Bolan wondered if exhaustion was catching up with him. He could have sworn that at least three men had trailed him to Washington National Airport, until he lost them in the crowded lobby.

It was time to take a little R & R and to forget about everything except relaxing and fishing. When this mission was finished, maybe he'd give his brother, Johnny, a call.

It was about time the two of them got together.

THE SLIM GRAY-HAIRED man sat on a bench in the Asheville airport lobby and studied the men and women who passed by. None of them interested him.

He was waiting for one man and knew exactly what he looked like. The sketch the client had provided showed the hard features of a man who could only be a mercenary.

The name Mike Belasko had been scrawled on the back, but that didn't mean a thing to him.

Felipe DeSantos checked his watch again—9:00 p.m. The plane was supposed to have landed ten minutes earlier.

There had been no activity at the Asheville airport for more than a hour. It was fall, and the tourist season was over. Only locals and those on business traveled to the small North Carolina town when the air began to chill.

He reached down and picked up the long nylon bag at his feet. He could feel the Uzi automatic rifle inside through the fabric. He'd received twenty-five thousand dollars in advance from his client, a senior military officer, to put together a team for this assignment.

The assassin didn't know why his client wanted to kill this Belasko, nor did he care. It was his business, not DeSantos's. All that mattered was that he'd been promised another twenty-five thousand if he was successful.

Compared to some of the jobs the client had given DeSantos when both were in Southeast Asia, this one was a breeze, and a lot more profitable.

He shut off his thoughts as he scanned the area and spotted the two men he had hired. Gripping the bags that contained the Uzis he'd provided, they were trying their best to blend into the crowd.

He had decided to make it look like a kidnapping. Let the local police and the FBI figure it out after he and his men escaped. It meant his team would have to kill more than just the target, but the resulting panic would make it easier for all of them to escape.

Killing came easy to DeSantos. He found out how good he was at it during the Vietnam War when he signed on as a mercenary and operated in Laos and Cambodia, and later in Central America.

He studied a tall, leanly muscled man in a windbreaker and black jeans, who walked down the corridor that led from one of the gates. Excitement coursed through DeSantos's body. It was him. His target.

The sheriff waiting outside the security gate was no problem. The revolver in the holster hanging from his belt was no match for the weapons the assassins carried.

DeSantos stood and gave his accomplices the signal, then moved to the back of the crowded terminal and opened his bag.

MACK BOLAN PAUSED at the bottom of the long ramp and studied the tall lean man who had a sheriff's badge pinned to his jacket.

The two men stopped and shook hands.

"Belasko?"

Bolan nodded.

"You Sheriff Handler?"

"Doug Handler. Thanks for coming."

"I'm told you can brief me on the situation," Bolan said.

"While we're driving back to Haywood," Handler promised.

Then saw the puzzled look on Bolan's face. "It's right next to the Great Smoky Mountains National Park."

"I've got a bag to pick up."

Because of security measures at airports, Bolan had to check his canvas carryall that contained his traveling arsenal with the captain of the flight. The federal ID, given to him by Brognola that made him a security adviser to the White House, stopped the airline officer from asking questions.

He decided to call Brognola first. It would take time for someone to lift the heavy bag and take it to the airline counter.

"I'll get the car and meet you out front," Handler said.

Bolan nodded and watched the sheriff disappear into the crowds. Handler had to have spent time in the military. He carried himself like a soldier.

The Executioner looked around for a telephone.

A bank of pay phones stood against the far wall, and he hurried toward them.

As he started to dial the cutout number that would eventually connect him to Brognola's desk at Stony Man Farm, his intuition, honed by years of battlefield experience, warned him of an impending threat. He hung up the phone and started to survey the large crowded room when he heard a commotion.

He turned and saw the frightened men and women cowering against the far walls of the terminal.

Then he heard a woman scream.

A skinny man in a casual jacket had rammed the muzzle of a 9 mm Uzi into the back of a well-dressed, frightened young woman and was demanding she walk in front of him.

The soldier wondered if it was a kidnapping. Public snatches weren't common, but they did happen.

His thoughts were diverted by an angry airport guard who pushed his way through the crowds, waving a Smith & Wesson 459 pistol.

It was suicide, Bolan thought, to confront a nervous gunman in a face-off challenge.

With little more than a casual glance, the gunman fired a short burst into the center of the dark uniform jacket. As the guard collapsed to the floor, Bolan's hand automatically went to shoulder leather. Then he remembered his weapons were waiting for him at the airline counter.

Hysteria ran through the terminal. Panicked men and women grabbed the hands of their families and pushed and shoved toward the exit doors, trampling anyone who came between them and escape.

Bolan ignored them and focused his attention on the gunman and his now hysterical hostage. With constant prodding from the lethal weapon in the small of her back, the woman kept moving toward the Executioner.

The antenna in his brain started sending danger signals. Without knowing why, the big man was now certain the gunman wanted him. He stood still until the hostage was almost next to him. The angry gunman shoved the woman aside and braced his body as he yanked back on the trigger of the submachine gun.

The Executioner waited until the killer started to fire the weapon before he took action. With the ease of years of practice, he lunged to the floor in a forward roll. Above him, he heard the burst of gunfire and the screams of the woman, then felt the splatter of her blood on his face as he sprang to his feet behind the hit man.

The cold-eyed thug twisted to face his mark. He triggered another sustained burst just as the soldier threw the point of his left boot into the surprised man's throat, then leaped out of the path of the lead-spewing muzzle.

Furious at the unexpected attack, the would-be assassin cursed as he continued to hose the space the American had just occupied.

An elderly couple who'd had the misfortune of being in the path of the searing slugs groaned and collapsed in each other's arms as lead tore into their bodies.

The Executioner rammed his knee into the killer's genitals. As the stunned man doubled over, Bolan slashed the callused edge of his right palm into his adversary's temple.

Openmouthed, the killer dropped his weapon. Ignoring it, Bolan rammed an elbow into the man's side, then followed up with a pointed thrust that ruptured the carotid artery in the neck.

While the dying hardman gagged on his own blood, Bolan snatched up the Uzi and turned quickly to see if there were any accomplices.

A young man, wearing the jeans and a sleeveless work shirt favored by biker gangs, charged at him, indiscriminately firing rounds from his Uzi at the fleeing crowd in front of him to clear his path. The soldier could hear the screams of people callously cut down by the death rounds.

Disciplined by years of experience to concern himself only with immediate danger, Bolan closed his mind to the cries of the innocent and dived behind a long bench.

Waiting until the attacker reached his cover, he rolled out, firing two short bursts at the gunman.

One of the rounds tore open the killer's throat. With a wide-eyed expression of confusion, he fell backward on top of the corpses he had created.

Grim-faced, the gray-haired leader of the trio grabbed a small blond child and held his Uzi against her head as he moved toward the front doors.

As Bolan raced toward him, the gunman released the girl, spun quickly and cut loose at the Executioner. But Bolan fired a sustained burst first.

The hit man stared at the line of bullet holes that stitched his chest, then collapsed to the floor.

The police would search through the pockets of the killers, but Bolan was certain they would find no identification. The three assassins were professionals.

Not good professionals, but professionals in any case.

As Handler rushed through the terminal door, Bolan hoped they could get this mess cleaned up in the shortest possible time.

CHAPTER TWO

Less than four hours earlier, Mack Bolan had been asked by Hal Brognola to join the President of the United States and him for a secret meeting in the Oval Office. Although he had long ceased to operate under the auspices of the government, the soldier knew that he wouldn't be summoned unless there was an emergency.

He could have said no, but Brognola had played a special role in Bolan's life. The head of the secret Sensitive Operations Group, based at Stony Man Farm, Virginia, had been more than just a liaison between the government and the team of antiterrorist commandos. He was one of the few men in government that the soldier trusted.

"Hal, I'm bone weary," Bolan remembered telling the head Fed. "I need some R & R."

"At least hear what the Man has to say," Brognola pleaded.

Bolan agreed to listen to what the President had to say.

The Executioner and Brognola were rushed to a private elevator and taken to the second floor of the White House. A Secret Service agent ran a metal-detector wand down the bodies of the two men, checking for hidden weapons, then led them to the Oval Office.

Two men had been waiting for them: the President and Alan Macomb, chief of staff.

The men shook hands briefly.

Macomb, a United States senator, had built a reputation for personal integrity when he headed the Senate's Select Committee on Organized Crime.

The President introduced the two new arrivals.

"Alan, I think you know Harold Brognola. At his behest, I have invited Mr. Mike Belasko to join us because of his experience in dealing with issues like the one we are about to discuss."

Acknowledging the introduction, the Executioner remembered how Macomb had studied him as he'd entered the room, obviously curious as to the credentials that had gotten the big man invited to the meeting.

Macomb didn't have time to ask any questions, because the President claimed their attention.

"Gentlemen, we face a problem that could destroy this country as completely as an attack by some enemy pounding us with nuclear weapons," the head of the government said.

He turned to his secretary. "Lillian, please take notes for the secure files."

The slim, handsome woman in her late thirties smiled and nodded.

"This country has been facing a series of challenges by hundreds of groups who would like to see the federal government destroyed or taken captive," the President began. "We know of nearly twenty thousand men and women who belong to them and actively participate in violent actions. And there is evidence that more than two hundred thousand people in this country actively support them—many using their business or political influence or donating substantial sums of money to help them stay in business."

Macomb arched an eyebrow. "That many? What kind of domestic antigovernment groups do we have in this country? Your basic militias?"

"Among others. Weekend soldiers in regional so-called armies with patriotic names. Bikers, like the White Aryan Resistance gang, skinheads, the

National Alliance, the Zionist Occupation Government—a particular brutal group that claims Jews dominate the federal government. Then there are groups with religious-sounding names, such as the CA, which stands for the Covenant, the Sword, the Arm of the Lord, the Tax Resisters Alliance, and so on," the President explained.

"That last one, I believe, was accused of planning to blow up Internal Revenue Service offices and other government facilities throughout the Southwest," Macomb commented.

"Not them, Alan," the President corrected. "But another group very similar to them. And there was no evidence against them that could stand up in court, so charges were dropped."

The President turned and looked at Brognola.

"Now at least we know who has been raiding our government arsenals."

"I wouldn't be surprised, Mr. President. All of them need weapons to carry out their personal vendettas.

The President turned to Macomb. "Do you have anything to add?"

The former senator opened his briefcase and took a folder. It was filled with a thick stack of pages to which he referred.

"There have been thirty documented attacks on

minorities and other groups by hate organizations in the past four months—the White Aryans, the various paramilitary militias—as they call themselves—fanatics against everything from federal taxes to abortions, to name a few. Not to mention the deaths of hundreds of innocents in the recent past in mass bombings of major government and public buildings by these same groups.''

The President's secretary had looked surprised. ''May I say something?''

The Man nodded.

He had high regard for Lillian Henshaw. She had spent years working on top security projects for the Joint Chiefs of Staff before the President had convinced her to work for him.

''The Constitution guarantees citizens the right of free speech and the right to bear arms,'' she reminded the President.

''What it doesn't guarantee is the right for these people to murder others who have a legal right to oppose their point of view,'' Macomb snapped. ''What I personally am for or against as far as moral issues are concerned isn't why we're here.''

''You're missing the point,'' the President said calmly.

Bolan was getting impatient with the bickering.

He turned to the tired-looking man behind the desk.

"What *is* the point, Mr. President?"

"The point is that we have reached a point in our history where various groups think that the only way to settle disagreements is by killing those who think differently or are different from them."

"How much is the government to blame for what's going on?" Macomb asked.

The President sighed. "Our citizens have always felt that the government has gotten too big, and that it has intruded too much into their personal lives. Perhaps we have. But whatever the reason, this country has never before been so subjected to the kind of organized violence it faces today."

"How can I help?" Bolan asked.

Macomb jumped into the conversation. "The President and those of us who are close to him have noted that there seems to be a common pattern emerging in much of the hate-inspired violence. Some of us who discussed this problem among ourselves believe that a number of the recent violent incidents are more than a coincidence."

The President leaned forward and picked up the conversation.

"That's where you come in, Mr. Belasko. I agree that people do feel the government is trying to control too much. But given the state of the country, if we didn't interfere, there might not be a country left. Can you help?"

"What do you expect me to do?"

"Whatever you determine is the best course of action. Based on what Hal has told me, and what I know personally, I am certain we can trust your judgment."

"Is there some particular group with whom you want me to start?"

Brognola jumped in with a comment. "I just received this from someone in the Justice Department," he said, handing the President a folder.

The Man studied the pages, then looked up at Brognola.

"Why would anyone want to do harm to the Montagnards? According to your notes, there are only a handful of them left in the world, and as I remember, they provided our troops with vital assistance once upon a time."

"Some people hate anybody who's different than they are," Brognola replied coldly.

The President handed a second folder to Brognola.

"An aide gave me this in the hallway. I haven't had a chance to read it, but he said it was information about a group that is being persecuted by..." He paused and glanced at the contents of the folder, then shook his head. "These two reports are about the same group—the Montagnards. So I guess it's the place to start. I'd appreciate your getting on this one immediately."

He turned to the others in the office.

"I recommend we form a small committee to meet regularly and review the situation, and Mr. Belasko's progress. The committee will include the three of us." He turned to Bolan. "Including you, of course, Mr. Belasko. Although I suspect you'll be too busy to come in for our meetings."

The President stopped.

"We should have a name for the committee."

Macomb jumped in. "Since this committee will be concerned with groups trying to splinter America, why not call it that—the Splinter Committee?"

The President thought about the name, then nodded. "Obviously, everything said or reported to the committee will be kept in total confidence."

He looked at the other three men and at his secretary. "Understood?"

She, like the others, nodded in agreement.

The President pushed his leather chair away from the large desk and stood.

The others in the Oval Office did the same.

The President started to leave, but stopped and turned back to face Hal Brognola.

"Don't wait for committee meetings, Hal. I want updates on this as often as you can get them to me. If I'm unavailable, leave the information with Lillian."

Then he turned to Mack Bolan. "Anything you need—information, equipment, assistance—request it through Hal and we'll get it to you.

"Good hunting," he added, "if that's the appropriate expression for wishing you luck."

As Lillian Henshaw, Macomb and the President left the Oval Office, the Man stated quietly, "Lillian, make a note that Mack Bolan is on the job."

Bolan turned to his old friend. "How far do you want to me go?"

Brognola weighed the question, then answered, "Officially, I can't tell you. But I believe there's more to this than a gang of pretend soldiers waving guns at a bunch of frightened refugees. Some place in the back of my brain, I have a notion that somebody—or a group of somebodies—is backing them. If you stop the crazies who call themselves the Carolina Militia, you might get other groups like them to think twice before taking action.''

He paused, then added, ''I guess what I'm saying is get down to North Carolina as fast as you can. Talk to this Sheriff Handler who contacted the Justice Department and find out where things stand between the Carolina Militia and the Montagnards. Then take whatever action you feel is necessary.''

CHAPTER THREE

The arsenal was a one-story structure erected on a secluded plot of land thirty miles outside Raleigh, North Carolina. A high, electrified fence surrounded the two-acre government property, and only a small sign identified the building as a military arsenal.

Inside, the oil-stained yellow forklift groaned as it lifted the heavy wooden crates of military assault carbines and slowly moved them through the cavernous warehouse to where Jim Banks, the night warehouse manager, stood.

"Get a move on, kid," Banks grumbled. "I'm not planning to spend all night watching you get tomorrow's shipments set up."

Perched on the hard seat of the vehicle, Pete Luria was getting fed up with the gray-haired man's complaints. For the two weeks he had been working there, all the old man had done was find fault with everything he did.

"I'm doing the best I can," he snapped back. "I'm sweating bullets as it is."

"Then take off your shirt and put some effort into your work so we can go home." The older man sounded cynical. "There ain't no girls around to make fun of your body."

The two armed uniformed guards broke out in laughter. He'd almost forgotten they were around. One of them was sitting on a wooden chair inside the barred security bay, while the other leaned against the opened side door to the loading dock.

Before the night was over, Luria promised himself he'd be the one laughing at them. Or at least at their dead bodies. Since he'd started working there, he'd been needled by Banks and the other warehouse workers about how much time he spent in the bathroom combing his hair.

If they knew he had a 10 mm Colt autopistol, loaded with 170-grain hollowpoint rounds, hidden under his shirt, they wouldn't be laughing. He wondered how the others would react to the tattoo carved on his shoulder, which read White Aryan Resistance in red-and-blue letters.

The three words spelled out the name of the

bike gang he had joined. Their initials explained what they believed in—war.

Lodge, the leader of the club, kept reminding the gang that they were in a struggle with various racial and religious minorities to survive. Even if it came to killing and robbery.

Luria knew the gang trusted him, even though he had been with them only a few months. Lodge himself had given Luria the Colt and showed him how to use it. With a muzzle velocity of 1300 feet per second, it was almost 150 feet per second faster than a conventional 9 mm handgun.

Luria had gone through a hellish initiation to earn the right to wear the tattoo.

This was his first assignment as a member of the gang.

"How about me taking a short break, boss?" Luria asked.

"Not until you get the rest of those stacks lined up for the pickups."

"Aw, c'mon…"

"Don't bitch to me. You're the one who begged me to let you pick up some extra money working overtime tonight. If it wasn't for your old man and me being friends for so many—"

"Okay," the long-haired young man said, interrupting him. "Where do you want this stack to go?"

Banks pointed to the chalked outline of a rectangle on the concrete floor. "Right here, where I wrote the shipping numbers."

Luria eased the forklift over the chalk marks and lowered the lift to the ground. The chain on the lift slipped, and the boxes made a loud noise as they landed.

The slim young man on the forklift hadn't busted his back for Lodge and the others to become a warehouseman. His old man had worked in a warehouse for thirty years before he died of a heart attack, and all it got his mother was a lousy small pension check every month.

In a way, he was grateful to his dead father. Even with the faked military records Lodge had somehow gotten, he wouldn't have been hired so quickly if Banks and the old man hadn't been personal friends for so many years.

Luria stopped the forklift and waited while Banks checked the stamped numbers on the crates against a manifest he held in his hand. Satisfied that the numbers matched, the supervisor pointed to where he wanted the crates placed.

"Watch what the hell you're doing!" Banks

shouted angrily. "Them ain't cotton puffs you're bouncing."

"I know what they are," Luria answered wearily. The markings on the crates were self-explanatory. They were filled with the latest version of the Colt M-16 A-2 assault carbines, and ammunition for them. As best he could calculate, he'd already moved more than twenty-five hundred guns and at least two hundred thousand rounds of ammunition.

"You bounce them the wrong way, and you could blow us all to hell," Banks added.

"Lay off, Jim," the guard inside the security bay called out. "You gotta first load those babies with ammo before they can cause trouble."

Luria smiled to himself. Before morning, the White Aryan Resistance would have enough guns and ammo to raise a lot of hell. All thanks to his hard work. Of course, most of them would be sold, but he was sure they'd keep a few crates for themselves. He could see Lodge patting him on the shoulder for the good work.

"Get the next load so we can start thinking about going home," Banks said, the fatigue evident in his voice as he worked his way past the forklift.

Load after load, Luria absorbed the verbal

abuse the older man kept dumping on him. As the hours passed, the two other warehousemen who were working overtime waved good-night as they were leaving.

"Hey, Luria," one of them called out as the guard near the door checked his ID badge. "I didn't see you comb your hair for more than an hour. Worried about it falling out?"

The biker hated being teased. Especially by assholes like these. There was nothing wrong with making sure his hair was combed and neat.

The other warehouseman laughed. "Stand you a beer before you head home," he told the first man.

"You're on," the wisecracker said, and the pair left.

Luria took a deep breath, then turned to the sweating old man who was staring angrily at him.

He kept thinking about the leader of the bikers. Lodge should have been here by now. Knowing how the man operated, Luria was certain he would show up when he was good and ready, and not before.

The gang leader was like nobody he'd ever met before. He stood six foot two and looked like a reincarnation of the Devil.

Luria had been told by some of the members

that Lodge had been in Vietnam and had gotten a taste for killing over there. A few of the bikers implied that the gang leader had been given a psycho discharge when his CO found the scalps of dead Cong hanging in the hut Lodge had called home.

He had seen Lodge take a dislike to someone without provocation and twist the man's head with his hands until his neck was broken without interrupting a conversation he was having with someone else.

All Luria really knew about the head of the club was that he had powerful government connections. Every so often, he would get a call from Washington, D.C., tipping him off to a new inventory of weapons or steering him to customers—usually antigovernment white supremacist groups.

Luria asked Banks a question. "What's the big rush about these guns, boss?"

"Replacements for the Pine Bush Arsenal," Banks replied. They had to ship their inventory off to Colombia. Something to do with the President promising guns to help knock off the drug barons down there."

Luria nodded. Privately, he was rooting for the drug dealers. Without the good stuff they shipped, most of the gang's parties would have been pretty boring. No way to get the gang's "mamas" turned on to a wild night of partying without an ample supply of coke. Especially that hot biker groupie, Mary Ellen, who had been given to him by Lodge.

He could still feel the incredible excitement that had coursed through him the last night he was with her. He remembered how sweet her freshly washed hair smelled. And how good she was in the sack.

"Now get those six crates from the security bay and put them here," Banks added, pointed to a chalked outline he was drawing.

Wearily, the frustrated younger man spun his forklift and headed for the security area.

"And be damned careful with them. They can go off if you shake them too much," the older man shouted.

The guard pressed a switch and let the gate slide open." You think it's smart to take these crates out before the special truck comes to pick it up, Jim?"

"I was assuming both of you were going to be on duty all night," Banks replied sarcastically. "You afraid you can't handle any big bad men who try to steal them?"

Embarrassed, the guard stepped aside and let Luria roll his vehicle into the barred area.

Carefully, Luria positioned his forklift next to the stack of wooden crates and worked the teeth of the vehicle under the stack. He turned to Banks. "What's so special about these boxes?"

"They're some kind of new 84 mm rockets developed by the Marine Corps that the infantry's going to test. The launchers for them are packed in the same cases. Just be gentle when you move them."

He eased his foot off the brake and started to move out of the security bay when he heard the muffled sound of bikes. Trying to hide his growing excitement, Luria forced himself to remain calm.

"What's taking you so damned long?" Banks snarled.

"I don't want to shake up the rockets in these—"

The guard near the door interrupted him. "Any of you hear that weird noise outside?"

"What noise?" Luria asked, forcing himself to look puzzled.

"Yeah," the guard in the security bay answered as he pressed the button to slide the heavy bar door shut and stepped out of the enclosed area to join the other armed man.

Luria heard a rapid sequence of explosions. Lodge and the others had arrived. He hoped they remembered to bring a truck big enough to transport all the crates he had moved.

Banks shouted to the guard at the door, "Hit the alarm!"

Luria jumped from the forklift and yanked out his 10 mm Colt pistol. Facing the door guard, he pumped two shots into his chest. With a muzzle energy that was twice that of a .45ACP, the hollowpoints tore two huge craters in the man's chest. As the guard slid down the wall against which he had been leaning, the slender gang member spun and pumped two hollowpoints at the second guard.

A fountain of blood spurted from the uniformed man's neck and left eye as he tried unsuccessfully to lift his M-16 A-2 to his shoulder, before he fell, facedown, to the painted concrete floor.

Jim Banks stared at the fallen bodies, then turned to Luria. "What the hell are you—"

The younger man stopped his question with three shots to his stomach. The gray-haired supervisor tried to stuff his intestines back inside, then gave up and collapsed to the floor.

The burst of rage continued to pour through Luria's body. He aimed the weapon at the motionless body of the hated foreman and squeezed the trigger again. The loud click of metal on metal enraged him. He dropped the empty gun and yanked the assault rifle from the hands of the dead security guard.

Standing over Banks, Luria pressed the rifle against the gasping man's ear and squeezed the trigger. The younger man shuddered for a moment as he watched bits of soft brain tissue and cartilage shoot from the ruptured head cavity. Then he walked to where the guards had fallen, intending to drill them with a few more rounds to guarantee they were dead.

"Hey, Hawkeye, they're dead. Don't go wasting ammo."

Luria recognized the voice and turned his head in its direction. It was Lodge, standing in the open doorway, grinning.

As he always did in the gang leader's presence, Luria backed away from him as if he were afraid to get too close. The gang leader's dark, deep-set eyes seemed to have a life of their own.

Lodge was huge. He looked as if he weighed more than three hundred pounds. His massive body seemed to spread in all directions, dominating every place he went. As usual, he was dressed entirely in black, except for the gang's symbol, which was stenciled in white on the T-shirt he wore.

Poker and Sterno, Lodge's two chief lieutenants, stood behind the man. Sterno was his closest friend; Poker was the club's executioner.

Right behind them was Connection, the kid the gang leader treated like his own younger brother.

Connection was younger than most of the others in the gang. What made him important to the gang was that he seemed to know exactly where to find drugs no matter where they were. It was as if Connection could smell who was dealing drugs, even in the middle of nowhere.

"Good work, kid," the huge man said, dropping his thick hand around Luria's shoulder. "What've we got?"

Luria pointed to the stacks of crates. "Those are all brand-new Colt M-16 A-2s." Then he pointed to another row of crates. "And those are filled with ammo for them."

The younger man saw a truck backing up to the loading dock. "Nice truck," he commented.

"Almost brand-new," Connection replied. "It's even got a CB radio."

"Guy who owned it won't be bullshitting with

other truckers where he's gone,'' added a man named Dirt Bag, laughing sarcastically.

Lodge turned to his men. "Let's get these crates loaded and blow this pop stand." He looked at the forklift. "And load this thing, too. We can use it later."

"I got us a bonus," Luria told the gang leader. He pointed to the stack of crates he'd moved from the security bay. "Some kind of new rockets. Really powerful. The launchers for them are packed in the same crates."

"We can talk about them later," Lodge said.

"Yeah," Sterno added. "Let's move. We ain't gonna be alone for long."

Sixteen more WAR bikers poured into the warehouse, walking past the bleeding bodies as if they were invisible.

Lodge turned to the rest of the gang. "Let's get the stuff loaded up. We got a customer with hard cash ready to pay for them."

Luria decided this was a good time to remind his leader what a good job he had done for the gang.

"Pretty big haul I got us," Luria bragged.

"I got the tip. All you did was shove some boxes around," Lodge said as he slipped a hand to his waistband. Swiftly, he pulled out a long stiletto and jabbed it into Luria's belly and pushed it upward until the man's entrails pushed through the stomach wall.

Luria was stunned. He could feel he was dying.

The gang leader pulled out the bloody stiletto and let Luria fall to the floor. "You're supposed to wait for me to tell you that you did a good job. Not you me."

He faced the rest of the gang, who stared at him. "The cops would have figured that he was the inside man if he came with us. This way, they'll have a hell of a time trying to find out who did it."

The gang members grinned. As always, Lodge made good sense.

The brutal, tattooed man turned to Connection. "Get in touch with those contacts of yours. We're gonna need us a mess of happiness stuff as soon as we get this stuff delivered."

Connection grinned happily. "We gonna party after we make the delivery?"

"Soon as you get us some stuff."

"Just tell me where we're heading, and I'll make some calls."

Lodge liked the kid. But he was still too new with the gang to be completely trusted with their destination.

"You know anybody along the interstate with some high-quality stuff we can pick up on the way?"

"Soon as we get to a pay phone, I'll make a few calls."

Lodge slapped him on the shoulder. "Don't disappoint me, kid."

"Have I ever, boss?"

The gang leader grinned coldly. "Not yet." Then added, "Okay, let's get the stuff loaded on the trucks. We got a long way to drive before we can collect our money and have us a party."

CHAPTER FOUR

This was not home. Not to Ha-Dock, the elder in the small community. As he stared at the stars beginning to emerge in the sky, he thought about how different this place was from where his ancestors had lived for more than a thousand years.

There were no tigers or other animals prowling in the night, the only clue to their presence their deep coughs and growls.

Rice wine had been replaced by another beverage. There was much foliage. Soft pine, hemlock, conifers and many other tree species were plentiful, but no banana trees, from which most of the houses in his ancestral homeland were built. But they were so far away from that place that it wasn't practical to have them shipped here.

Beef from cows had replaced the buffalo meat on which Ha-Dock and the others had feasted. There were chickens and rice, but the rice was strange, not the glutinous grains that had been part of the daily diet.

The short sleeveless tunics covering loincloths worn by the men, and the skirts and long-sleeved tunics the women wore had been replaced by Western clothing. Now the men wore jeans or khaki shorts, and the women covered their bodies in styles acquired from Sears and JC Penney catalogs.

Even though some of the men and women still smoked the long pipes, many had abandoned the custom. Especially the younger ones, who were exposed to reports they heard on television and to what they learned in school.

Certainly, the commune on which the group lived was comfortable and adequately stocked with cattle, chicken and pigs. And the soil was fertile. But it wasn't home. Home was many thousands of miles away. In the highlands of Vietnam. But their village was now occupied by soldiers of the North Vietnamese Army.

The elderly man puffed on his pipe and stared down the slope of their hilltop commune. What was left of the once-flourishing Montagnards now lived where once only Cherokee Indians dwelled. There were more different kinds of trees than in all of Southeast Asia, but none like those in his homeland.

Where the one-time mountain dwellers of Vietnam had scratched the soil to raise crops for their own use, luxuriant plant life flourished, in a summer display of almost every color in the rainbow.

On the edge of the Oconaluftee Valley, the refugees had been given a tract of land where they could raise their crops, their pigs and their families without fearing an attack by the Vietcong or the North Vietnamese Army. Still fearful of strangers after all this time, the Montagnards rarely left their community, except to see a doctor or purchase essential supplies.

Asheville, North Carolina, was an hour away by car. But except for the day they had landed there to begin their journey into the Great Smoky Mountains, the older Southeast Asian natives had never seen the city.

Even Haywood, the county seat and a twenty-minute drive away, was rarely visited. Members of the community occasionally drove through the mountains to see how the Montagnards were faring, but mostly they were left in peace.

They were the last of the tens of thousands of hill tribesmen the French had nicknamed the Montagnards when they had occupied the Southeast Asian lands. That wasn't their real name. They were the Dega—the first people of the country known as Vietnam. The tales the elders handed down had said they had occupied the highlands of Southeast Asia for thousands of years before the Chinese to their north had chased many of the tribes into the lands now known as Vietnam, Laos, Cambodia, Myanmar and Thailand.

Ha-Dock dreamed they would some day be able to return to their highlands. Perhaps even before he died. This was the promise the spirits of the forest had given them when they bade farewell and left to escape the NVA, the Pathet Lao and the Khmer Rouge.

Thousands of the fierce warriors had been slaughtered by the Communist-led troops until the last several hundred had been rescued by the same Americans whom they had protected—sometimes with their own bodies—and were flown to North Carolina where a large charity organization had purchased a tract of farmland on the edge of the Great Smoky Mountains.

Assimilating had been difficult, Ha-Dock remembered as he puffed on his long homemade pipe and stared at the stars shining down from the sky.

Not only for them but their neighbors.

All they wanted was to be left alone to build long communal structures mounted on stilts as they had in Vietnam. But the local laws insisted they construct more permanent housing.

Stilt-house construction would have been difficult, Ha-Dock remembered, without the large groves of bamboo that had flourished in Southeast Asia. Here they had to build their communal structures out of soft pinewood.

Their neighbors believed they were Vietnamese—a culture the Dega despised. Their children were taunted in school because of their looks and lack of formal education. Some of the men in the nearby town of Hilltop kept calling them "Charlie," a nickname the Americans had given to the North Vietnamese guerrilla fighters.

If anything, the Dega hated the Vietcong even more than the Americans did. The guerrilla warriors had stolen their food and raped their women before murdering entire villages.

Because of the language difference, only the handful of Americans who had sponsored their relocation years earlier understood who and what the hill tribes were.

Haywood County Sheriff Doug Handler did. He'd been an American Special Forces captain in

Vietnam, and he'd been a friend to them for many years.

But he and the few like him were like blades of grass trying to fight the storm of the hate and mistrust of the others who lived near and around them.

Lately, strange fires had been started on their land. Their houses had been spray-painted with strange words a number of times. Only the children of the village who understood English could translate them.

"Go home, Charlie, before it's too late!"

As Ha-Dock continued to stare at the sky, he whispered the prayer the Christian missionary who had converted the villagers had taught them.

"Forgive us as we forgive them," he started to say.

Then he heard the sounds of gunfire.

These weren't the rifles the Dega men kept for hunting game. These were combat weapons. Loud, rapid firing.

Ha-Dock had heard them in Vietnam. He could see the flashes of burning cordite as bullets tore into the handful of communal houses.

Men, women and children were screaming with pain. Ha-Dock saw several of the men rush from the long houses carrying rifles. But before they could raise them to their shoulders, he watched in horror as their bodies absorbed lead from the weapons of war.

He could see men in combat fatigues firing their carbines as they rushed forward. But he couldn't see their faces, as they were covered by ski masks.

But why were soldiers firing at the Dega? What had they done wrong?

He would never ask the question of his killers. A pair of 5.56 mm rounds drilled through the outer layer of wrinkled skin that covered his face and rammed into his brain.

The village elder fell facedown into a pool of his gore just as a half-dozen masked attackers tossed grenades into the houses.

The flimsy structures tore apart, showering the fields with bits of blood and tissue from the Montagnards who had been hiding inside the houses.

A LARGE, HULKING FORM stopped one of the masked fighters.

"How many does that make, Rich?"

"I counted thirty-nine, Colonel. That's not including anybody inside those huts these Commies built," the hooded killer replied in a youthful-sounding voice.

"Maybe now they'll finally get the message that we don't want them in our country," one of the other masked shooters commented.

A swarm of ski-masked men joined them. Each carried one of the latest versions of the Colt M-16 A-2 carbine.

"Do you think we got them all, Colonel?"

Everyone in the militia called Larry Potter "colonel." The owner of the huge military-surplus warehouse on the edge of Haywood was their undisputed commander, and founder of the Carolina Militia.

Potter pulled the ski mask from his head. His face was scarred with pockmarks from a child-hood illness. He ignored the question and turned to two of the hooded men.

As they yanked off their ski masks, he asked, "How many did you two get?"

Neither answered. Potter pushed his M-16 A-2 against the first man's face.

"How about you, Eddie?"

Sweating, Eddie moved back a few steps. His bright red hair was thick and matted from the per-spiration of wearing the knitted hood.

"I don't...don't know. I was too busy," he stuttered.

The gun dealer turned to the second man.

"How many did you shoot, Billy Joe?"

Shivering, the dark-haired young man answered nervously. "I didn't get a chance to count. Eddie and me, we were too busy."

"Now the two of you will get a chance to kill the rest of these Commies who didn't die, and their sympathizers."

"What sympathizers, Colonel?"

The question was asked by a blond man with a long scar that crossed his face at an angle.

"I got a tip, Captain Holt," Potter said. "The Feds have hired a mercenary to come down here and try to destroy the Carolina Militia."

He didn't add that the tip had come directly from the federal government. A career colonel named Timmons had been his contact with unknown government officials who sympathized with the goals of the Carolina Militia.

It had been through Timmons that he first met Marty Comer, the talk-radio celebrity, who supported the goals of antigovernment groups like the militia. And Timmons had helped Potter find the newest weapons for his troops.

He turned to the sixteen armed men. "I want you to stay here and get rid of the rest of these Commies. And take care of the mercenary if he actually shows up."

He turned to Holt.

"You're in charge, Captain. Get some of your men to fit them M-203 grenade launchers to their carbines. And use them!"

Then he added, "And get back to the camp as soon as you can."

He turned and started to walk toward the parked jeeps.

"Wait up, Colonel. I'm going back with you," Eddie said.

Potter turned his face toward the young gunman.

"What?"

"We've been able to scare them with the signs we painted on their buildings and starting fires. I don't think we got a right to kill them, too."

"I agree with Eddie," the frightened dark-haired youth stated. "What are they going to find? A bunch of dead Commies. There's been enough killing. All of us should get out of here and pretend we don't know anything if they show up."

"I didn't sign up with this outfit to kill some unarmed Orientals," the red-haired youth said loudly, searching for the strength to overcome his fear of Larry Potter. "I'd do anything to get these Commies out of our country, but I don't see any reason for killing women and little babies."

"When I was in Nam, the government had ways of making a man talk against his will. They got drugs they shoot into your arm to make you babble like a baby," the head of the militia said. "They'll get you to tell them everything about the militia you swore to keep secret."

"They couldn't make either of us talk, Colonel. I swear," Billy Joe pleaded.

"In the Army, they call this insubordination. You know the penalty for that?"

Eddie nodded, forcing a smile on his face. "Yeah, but this isn't the real Army."

Sighing, the older man in fatigues drew the .45-caliber Colt Government Model pistol in the leather holster he wore. He raised the weapon and fired two rounds at Eddie's chest.

Blood spurted out the multipatterned fatigue shirt and spread across the young man's chest. Still looking stunned, Eddie stared at the leader of the militia and tried to ask a question.

"Why did you...?"

He fell to the ground before he could finish.

In shock, the black-haired young man stared at the body. He lifted the M-16 A-2 in his hand and started to point it at the older man.

Calmly, Potter emptied the clip in his pistol into Billy Joe's face. The youth's skull exploded into a shower of splintered bones, torn skin and shredded brain matter as he fell to the ground next to his friend.

"That's what we did to soldiers who wouldn't obey orders. I can't tolerate insubordination," Potter told the rest of the men in a quiet voice. "Somebody cover their bodies. They might have been cowards, but they tried to be good soldiers."

Potter eased the weapons from the pair's bloody, still hands and slowly climbed the hill.

As he neared his jeep, the head of the Carolina Militia wondered what effect the deaths of Eddie and Billy Joe would have on the rest of the men.

Then he decided it would be a good reminder to them that they were at war with the Feds, and not just having fun and playing games.

CHAPTER FIVE

Doug Handler had planned to turn over supervision of the sheriff's office in Haywood to one of his men while he went home and prepared himself dinner. He had scheduled a quiet evening in front of the television set, and going through the old photo albums to remember the life he had shared with his wife, Eloise, before her death from cancer a year earlier.

Then, out of the blue, a call had come saying that a federal investigator was on his way to check out the situation with the Montagnards.

As they drove toward the county seat from the airport, Handler started to ask the man questions about his government position, but Bolan cut him off with a question of his own.

"How do I get to the Montagnards' farm commune?"

"Why?"

"I want to see the area around their land."

"What's that got to do with stopping these threats?"

Bolan looked at the local law-enforcement officer coldly. "Then I want to see where this Carolina Militia makes its headquarters."

Handler sensed that the visitor from Washington, D.C., knew exactly what he was doing.

"For the most part, they're just a bunch of loudmouths who like to make a lot of noise. Especially when they're drinking."

"Who heads up the group?"

"Guy named Larry Potter. He pretends he's a colonel. He owns a military-surplus warehouse on the edge of town. I'd shut him down, but he was smart enough to locate his place just across the county line."

"What about getting that sheriff's assistance?"

"Jeff Rusher?" Handler had a look of disgust on his face. "No way. First of all, he's as much a racist as Potter and his men. Second, I have a strong hunch Rusher makes a good buck peddling weapons he's obtained illegally to people like Potter."

"Why 'colonel'?" Bolan asked.

"Gave it to himself. Potter made it to sergeant in some infantry company in Vietnam before he got shot in the ass running away from a surprise attack by the Vietcong. He demanded the Army give him a Purple Heart for his wounds.''

Bolan studied the sheriff, then asked, ''You seem to know a lot about this Potter. How come?''

Handler smiled. ''I was his commanding officer in Nam. Tried to get him kicked out of the Army for insubordination until he got himself shot and grabbed a medical discharge.''

''Any chance this Rusher provided the Carolina Militia with their artillery?''

''He isn't big-time enough to come up with that many guns. And mostly he peddles used military weapons, not brand-new ones.''

Bolan made a decision. ''I guess the place to start is to talk to the Montagnards and find out firsthand what's been going on.''

There was something no-nonsense about the man. The sheriff knew Belasko was different than any of the federal people he had previously met.

''Well, let's go.''

''It's not your job to take me there,'' Bolan reminded him. ''I can rent a car.''

''It's not an easy place to find, and the Montagnards are suspicious of strangers. Especially since they've been receiving threats.''

He glared defiantly at Bolan. "Besides, anything criminal that happens in Haywood County is my job. I don't know what agency you're really with—FBI, CIA or some secret group the government has created—but this is my county. And I make the decision who and what gets protected or arrested."

Bolan studied the law officer.

"And your decision about me?"

"I'm sticking like glue until you leave Haywood County."

What bothered Handler most was the gun Belasko wore in a shoulder holster under his camouflage hunting jacket. The sheriff was sure the federal agent had a permit for carrying it concealed. And since many men in the country toted handguns, it wasn't unusual for visitors to do the same.

But why, Handler wondered, did Belasko need to carry one?

Unless he was with the Immigration and Naturalization Service—the government agency that found illegal immigrants and kicked them out of the country—and thought he might have to protect himself from the Montagnards.

It was a question like the one he had never gotten around to asking the visitor. About what agency he worked for. Now, the sheriff reminded himself, he had two questions to ask when the opportunity became available. Who did Belasko represent and why did he carry a gun.

As they drove through the county seat and headed for Highway 74, Handler glanced at the long canvas bag Belasko had brought with him. The bulky man didn't dress like a fashion plate. In fact, Belasko was the first federal representative Handler had met who hadn't shown up wearing a well-tailored suit and tie. Quite the contrary. The visitor was wearing boots, jeans and a wool-lined hunting jacket.

His sudden appearance still bothered Handler. Was he here to tell the Southeast Asian refugees they had to leave the United States?

Had the antiimmigrant groups finally reached the ear of the President? There was no place for the survivors to go. Not Vietnam, where they faced certain death. If it came to it, Handler made up his mind, he would fight off any efforts to kick the Montagnards out of the country. Even if he had to resort to using a gun to do it.

He stared out the window. The light in the sky was fading. He hoped Belasko would be done with his business before dark. Highway 74 was hell to maneuver on at any hour. At night it was almost suicidal.

Handler pointed to a dirt road on the left.

"We turn here. If you think 74 is hell, the dirt road makes it look like an interstate highway."

Handler slowed and inched his way onto the unpaved roadway.

"What do you expect to find here, Mr. Belasko?"

"Maybe nothing, if I'm lucky. We'll see."

They moved slowly on the narrow road. Handler pointed to dark shadows ahead of them. "The farm's just around the bend."

As they turned around a corner, the soldier saw partial structures, but no people.

Handler honked the horn, then looked puzzled.

"Something's wrong. The kids usually rush up to say hello."

Handler stopped the Bronco and started to open the door.

Bolan agreed with the sheriff. Something *was* wrong. He could sense danger.

"Wait," Bolan told him, reaching over the seat to grab his canvas carryall.

He was too late. Handler had already gotten out from the vehicle.

A barrage of high-velocity explosions from

fired ammo temporarily lit a section of woods and shattered the eerily still night. One of the rounds tore into the sheriff.

Handler tumbled to the ground and rolled over, facedown.

The Executioner's impulse was to jump out of the Bronco and rescue the fallen lawman, but his combat instincts held him back.

At least until he was ready to face the hidden enemy.

Bolan opened the canvas bag that contained his portable arsenal and grabbed a silenced Uzi submachine gun and three full magazines, as well as the .44 Magnum Desert Eagle semiautomatic pistol.

He mounted a sheath onto his forearm that contained a razor-sharp Applegate-Fairbairn double-edged combat knife. The Desert Eagle was already seated in its rigid holster, which was mounted on a webbed belt ready to be anchored to Bolan's waist.

He also pulled a combat vest from the bag. Quickly, he attached a half-dozen 40 mm fragmentation grenades and extra ammo clips for the silenced Beretta 93-R that rode in shoulder leather, as well as clips for the Desert Eagle.

Now it was time for the battle to really begin.

The Executioner slipped out of his jacket and jeans, revealing his blacksuit. The sight of the big man in black was intimidating to many hardened criminals. It was as if he were an agent of death.

For many of those he confronted, he was.

Like the shadows who had been waiting for the sheriff and him.

How did they know the two of them were coming?

That was a question that would have to wait until he had sent the hidden killers to meet whatever God they had.

Slipping on the combat vest, anchoring the web belt to his waist and shouldering the Uzi, the Executioner knew the first strike had just started. Now it was up to him to show the enemy how war was supposed to be fought.

CHAPTER SIX

"The shots must have killed the sheriff and the mercenary the Feds sent here," the youngest of the militiamen told his three companions as he pulled his hood from his head.

The young man, barely past his teens, wore a frightened expression as he tried to stare into the open fields past the woods where they were hiding.

"And a waste of ammo if you ask me, Ned. We could have taken out the two of them with half the shots we fired," a second gunner growled as he removed his ski mask to reveal the face of an angry-looking man in his late forties. "You kids got to learn that ammo costs the militia money. But you're right. Both those guys are dead," he admitted.

"Maybe they are, Daryl. But let's be careful. They could still be alive," the leader of the quartet warned as he removed the mask that had covered his head and face.

The first of the group looked worried. "You really think so, Captain Holt? What do we do now?"

Gary Holt was one of the commanders of the Carolina Militia, outranked only by Potter and his aide, Colonel Johnny Skeeters.

"Wait."

"For what?"

"For a couple of you men to check and see if the two are dead," Holt said, pointing to a pair of militiamen. "Let me know what you find."

"I'm not hanging around," Daryl said arrogantly. "If they're alive, they're badly injured. We're four. They're only two. And we have lots of other men looking for anybody still alive on this farm. I say we finish them off. If need be, I'll go by myself."

Reluctantly, Holt gave in and ordered the others to gather their weapons.

"We'll search for them in teams of two," the militia commander ordered.

They paired off and moved cautiously into the forest.

TIGHTENING HIS GRIP on the Uzi SMG, Bolan scoured the nearby areas, searching for signs of life. He was sure that he had lessened the possibility of being seen by wearing the blacksuit. What he wasn't sure of was if the sheriff was dead or alive. But this wasn't the time to think about it.

Bolan saw nothing moving in any direction. Then two shadows separated from the shadowy stands of hardwood trees.

A pair of shadows tried to use the brush as a blind while they crouched on their haunches and worked their way past the stand of oak and walnut trees the soldier was using for cover.

The first of the shadows sprinted for the bushes on Bolan's left. He suspected the assailant wasn't sure where his target was hiding, but only had a sense of the general area.

The Executioner could make out the 5.56 mm M-16 A-2 slung over a shoulder. For a split second, he wondered how the gunman had gotten his hands on one. The military weapons weren't in general distribution.

He slipped the Applegate-Fairbairn combat knife from its thin leather sheath and waited patiently until the figure came closer. Then Bolan moved behind a thick stand of foliage. As the attacker moved past him, the Executioner clamped a hand over the man's mouth.

A quick slash across the militiaman's neck carved a bloody grin across his slender throat. Easing the still form to the ground, Bolan heard the faintest hint of a noise behind him. Whipping the Beretta from its holster, he spun and unleashed a pair of 9 mm rounds that punched through the second man's sternum, ruptured one of his lungs and exploded the heart muscle. Only a short grunt of pain and a small geyser of blood from severed blood vessels announced the end of his life.

The Executioner was in no mood to play cat and mouse with the enemy force hidden in the forest around him. He didn't know how many there were or where they were hiding. It was time to flush them.

Moving behind a boulder, Bolan pulled a frag grenade from the combat vest and lobbed it like a small football into the bushes in front of him. Flattening himself against the leaf-padded ground, he could hear the explosion of the missile and shrieks of the dying and wounded as burning shards of metal tore into hidden assailants.

Tossing a second grenade to his left, Bolan waited for the slivers of burning metal to shred human tissue, then rose into a crouch and sprinted twenty yards to his left.

A third thrown grenade exploded and scattered another group of hidden militiamen. Except for the cries of pain echoing in front of him, there was no hint of movement.

The Executioner waited patiently, making sure none of the attackers was watching for him to expose himself. For ten minutes, he waited to see who, if anyone, moved out from behind the thick shrubbery.

Suddenly, the forest around exploded with fury. From all sides, Bolan heard the crackling of gunfire. Bullets tore into the trees and bushes but miraculously missed him.

A soft movement on his left got his attention. Two men in military fatigues raced into the open space in front of him. Both, the soldier noted, were dripping blood as they charged, their faces covered with expressions of terror.

From experience, Bolan knew that fear could pump up the adrenaline and move fighters to irrational actions. It would take more than a well-placed pair of slugs to stop the two tearing toward him.

The soldier stood and waited for the duo to get closer, then he washed them with the full anger of the rounds in the Uzi magazine. The slugs ripped apart the throat of the closer charger, nearly severing his head from his body, while the second, the taller of the two, clutched his midsection, trying to stop his exposed intestines from oozing onto the ground.

Bolan rammed a fresh clip into the Uzi and waited.

The second attacker pulled his hands away from his ruptured body and pointed his M-16 at where Bolan had been standing. In one last desperate effort, he jammed his finger against the trigger of the carbine and emptied the clip. The force of the recoil shoved him backward. He fell to the ground and lay there, his blood soaking into the vegetation around him.

Battle-wise, the soldier had moved after he emptied his clip so the 5.56 mm slugs from the M-16 tore holes into the thick brush instead of into him.

Bolan wasn't sure who had sent the hit squad, but he knew this wasn't the time to worry about it. Right now, he had to find out if any of the militiamen remained alive.

Four shadows ran into the dense underbrush. Weighing his options, the soldier yanked a frag grenade from the combat vest. Pulling the pin, he lobbed the bomb toward the fleeing gunmen.

Cries of agony from the underbrush pierced the quiet night. The Executioner waited until an assailant, fatigues and flesh scorched from the superheated fragments of metal shards, staggered out of the deep brush.

Clenching his carbine, the crazed attacker fired wildly, then turned the gun on himself, chiseling a 5.56 mm hole in his skull, spilling scrambled brains down his slumping body.

Now the Executioner knew what kind of adversaries he was facing. Not the best combat soldiers, but men who would rather kill themselves than face capture.

The soldier scouted the surrounding brush, searching for signs of surviving gunmen. He could see none. But some sixth sense warned him he wasn't alone. He moved forward and triggered his Uzi, aiming at the low brush. Nine millimeter hollowpoints shredded the bushes, but there were no cries of pain, no hint of life.

Suddenly, an explosion behind him made Bolan turn.

A body collapsed to the ground. What was left of the militiaman's face was covered by a mask of blood and torn tissues.

Sheriff Handler stood over the body, holding his .357 Magnum Colt Python revolver in his right hand. He studied the body, then lifted his head and looked at Bolan.

There was a puzzled look on the lawman's face as he stared at the blacksuit Bolan was wearing. The soldier saw that the sheriff had decided this wasn't the time to ask about it.

Blood dripped down the side of the lawman's face, and his mouth was clenched with pain.

"You missed one, Belasko," he said calmly. "He used to be Alf Jackson, one of the guys who hung around Larry Potter's military-surplus warehouse."

Then he fainted from his gunshot wound and fell to the ground.

CHAPTER SEVEN

Bolan knelt beside Handler and checked his wound. The 5.56 mm round had gouged a furrow of flesh from Handler's temple. As far as the warrior could tell, it was basically a flesh wound. But the sheriff had lost blood.

The lawman opened his eyes and looked up at Bolan.

"I need a hand up," he said weakly.

"Lie there. I'll use your radio and call for backup and an ambulance."

"I can't spare the manpower. If you're going to call anybody, radio the state police for backup. They've got a post forty miles from Haywood. And I don't need an ambulance."

Bolan didn't want the police to interfere. While he had a great deal of respect for cops, he found that too many of them were stuck with rules and regulations about what they could and couldn't do.

"Give me a hand," Handler repeated, then added, "Please."

Reluctantly, the soldier helped the lawman to his feet. Still shaky, the sheriff shook his head.

"I wonder where the Montagnards are."

"Maybe they ran into the hills when the gunfire started," Bolan suggested.

"Maybe," the sheriff agreed.

With Bolan's help, he wandered around the area. As he looked at the bodies of the attackers, he seemed disgusted.

"I know most of them," he commented. "Just the kind of malcontents you'd expect the Carolina Militia to enlist."

He stopped at a pair of bodies and seemed stunned.

"Dear God," he muttered as he studied their faces.

"Know them?"

"Too well. That one," he said, pointing to the body on the left, "is Billy Joe Fetterman, son of the mayor of Haywood. The one next to him— the redheaded kid—is Eddie Masterson, a jock on the University of North Carolina football team."

He shook his head. "What in the hell were these two doing here?"

"Trying to kill people they didn't like," Bolan commented bluntly.

Handler kept staring at them.

"I know both of them thought the federal government was trying to control their lives," he said, turning his head to look blankly at the Executioner. "A lot of us do. Sometimes the Feds act as if they can get away with anything. No accountability."

He became quiet. Then spoke again, his voice quavering with the shock of seeing the two young men's bodies. "But to team up with a bunch of thugs like the others..."

He didn't finish the sentence.

Bolan knew how he felt. One of the reasons he was no longer part of the government was the feeling some officials figured they didn't have to justify their actions to anybody. Only Hal Brognola understood how the soldier felt, even though he elected to stay with the federal government.

"Let's get you back to your vehicle so you can call in for ambulances and a paramedic. Then we can look for the Montagnards," Bolan suggested gently.

"Yeah. I guess that's what we should do," Handler agreed.

The conversation was interrupted by a loud whooshing sound coming toward them. Bolan shoved the sheriff to the ground and threw himself over the lawman.

"Keep your head down," he ordered.

The whining sound traveled past them and landed in a grove of trees. Handler started to get up, but Bolan pushed him down again.

"Stay down!"

The forest to the right echoed an explosion that sounded like a bolt of thunder. Large chunks of timber and branches were propelled in every direction by the force of the eruption. Flames began to consume the trees and the brush.

Bolan helped the sheriff to his feet, then asked, "Any injuries?"

Handler cautiously moved his body. "I don't think so."

Staring at the burning trees, Handler turned and looked at Bolan.

"How did you know?"

"I've heard the sound before—a grenade launched from an M-203 slung under an M-16."

"It's been a lot of years since I heard that sound." He looked back at the trees ignited by the frag bomb. "I guess not all of the Carolina Militia are dead."

"Wait here," Bolan ordered in a low voice as he unleathered the .44 Magnum Desert Eagle.

The Executioner worked his way through the brush, trying to keep the sounds of his movements to a minimum. He placed each foot carefully as he searched for the pocket of adversaries responsible for the grenade attack.

For a large man, Bolan was amazingly light-footed. Years of combat had equipped him with the skill of moving with the silence of a cat.

Listening intently, the soldier could hear hushed whispers beyond the thick row of tall bushes. He couldn't make out the words, but within minutes he had determined how many gunmen waited on the other side.

Two. Armed, he assumed, with automatic weapons, based on the fighters he had already destroyed.

He raised the massive Desert Eagle. Silence was no longer a consideration. Only death.

The two gunners. Or him.

NERVOUSLY, THE PAIR of fatigue-clad militiamen checked behind every tree before moving forward. They had seen the mass slaughter their intended victim had wrought on the other men.

Holt was glad that the enemy hadn't died. Not that he was against killing. He had killed too many to let that bother him. But he wanted to hand over the men to the colonel as a gift.

Then Potter could show the surviving troops how to execute the enemy.

"Let's follow this trail," Holt told his companion, pointing to a dirt path. "It leads to—"

His words were interrupted by the charging black-clad form.

Before they could shoulder their weapons, Bolan loosed a pair of .44-caliber rounds. The slugs shattered the face of the militia captain. Deflected by his thick jawbone, the lead ricocheted and drove bone splinters into the man's brain.

There was no time for crying out. Death was instant.

The Executioner wasted no time on the new corpse. He made a half turn and drilled a pair of lead killers into the second militiaman's heart.

Blood spurted from severed vessels and poured out of the newly created chest cavity.

Bolan paused to listen for evidence of any other militiamen. Sure enough, he could hear the rustle of brush and whispers as a trio of weekend warriors pushed through the thick undergrowth.

The Executioner wanted to keep one of the three alive for questioning. The other two were expendable. He took out two militiamen with dead-on head shots, then turned to the last living member of the squad.

The hard-faced warrior gestured for the terrified militiaman to drop his weapon. Slowly, the man bent and started to place his carbine on the ground. Then he suddenly raised it and started to yank back on the trigger.

Behind Bolan, a large-caliber handgun unleased its fury. Turning quickly, the soldier began to squeeze the trigger of the Desert Eagle, but held off when he saw the sheriff. The Colt Python was tightly gripped in his hand.

"He could have told us who sent him," Bolan growled.

"And you'd be dead," Handler replied.

"I guess I owe you my life," Bolan replied as he rammed a full magazine into the Desert Eagle.

"What's got me curious is where they got their weapons," Handler commented, picking up the M-16 A-2 the dead attacker was carrying. "Looks practically new."

The soldier took the weapon from the lawman,

quickly field-stripped it and inspected the various parts.

"I'd say it hasn't been fired before today," he observed. Looking up at Handler, he stated, "You can't buy these in gun shops around here."

"Right. They're automatic, so, they're illegal to own without a federal license. But where are they getting them?"

The Executioner didn't know. No more than he knew how the Carolina Militia ambusher knew when he was coming.

They were questions the soldier planned to put to Hal Brognola when he called him later.

CHAPTER EIGHT

Doug Handler stared down at the body of the elderly Asian man.

"He's dead," the sheriff announced, turning and staring at Bolan with disbelieving eyes. "Who would want to kill Ha-Dock? He was just an old man who never bothered anybody."

"You said there were nearly a hundred people on this farm. Where are the rest?"

The sheriff shook his head, then unleathered his Colt Python.

"That's what I'm going to find out," he replied grimly.

He turned and walked away from Bolan at a brisk pace. As he reached the buildings, he stopped and took in the shredded houses.

"Something blew up their communal houses," he said in a hushed whisper.

"Or someone," Bolan replied. "The men we killed."

Handler glanced at the 9 mm Uzi in the soldier's hand, then hurried up the steps of the closest house. Opening the door, he stood dumbfounded at the sight of the carnage in front of him.

Walls, ceilings and floors were splattered with the blood. Body parts were strewed across the large room. Gripping the large Colt in his two hands, the sheriff worked his way past the bodies and searched the adjoining rooms.

"Nobody here," he reported in a shaky voice. "No one alive."

Then he brushed past Bolan and went outside, where he leaned against one of the shattered buildings and retched.

Bolan understood how the sheriff felt. He hadn't known any of the refugees from Vietnam, but the sight of dead innocents had made his blood run cold.

Ignoring the pain he felt from his head wound, Handler moved away from Bolan toward the destroyed communal buildings. "I'm checking the other houses," he replied, holding the .357 Magnum in front of him, ready to fire.

The soldier followed him from building to building.

Bodies were all that he found in the other buildings—women, children, men. All dead, all torn apart by bullets from high-powered weapons.

Bolan followed the sheriff outside.

The whimpering of a child caught both men's ears. Handler raced to the stand of bushes and saw a three-year-old girl standing helpless, staring at the gun in his hands.

"It's okay," the sheriff said in a suddenly gentle voice. "Where is everybody?"

The child stared at Bolan, terrified at the gun in his hands.

"He's here to help me," Handler reassured her.

Suddenly, the small girl grabbed one of Handler's hands and led him behind the bushes.

A small group of terrified Montagnard men, women and children huddled together. As the two Americans moved toward them, the group recoiled.

Handler looked angry. "Who did this?"

A number of voices competed with one another for the sheriff's attention. Handler raised his hand.

"One at a time." He pointed to an elderly woman. "You first, Grandmother."

"Men came wearing masks and carrying weapons."

Bolan interrupted. "Masks?"

The woman nodded. "Masks woven together like baskets."

"Sounds like ski masks," Handler commented.

"Did you hear them speak?" Bolan asked.

The old woman nodded. "They spoke with your tongue."

"Did they use any names?"

The woman shook her head, but a young woman raised her hand.

Handler turned to her.

"They called one of them the title of one of your officers."

The sheriff was puzzled. "What kind of title?"

"You were a lieutenant in Vietnam. Someone more important."

"Captain?"

The woman shook her head.

"Colonel?"

Shaking in terror, the elderly woman slowly nodded.

Handler turned back to Bolan, his face filled with disgust. "Larry Potter."

"Are you sure?"

The lawman turned back to the frightened woman. "Did you see his face?"

She shook her head. "He and other men wear masks."

Bolan weighed the information. "Are there any other paramilitary groups in the area?"

"None I know."

"And you said some of the dead men belonged to Potter's group."

"I can't swear to that," Handler replied carefully. "What I'm sure of is that I saw some of the dead men spending a lot of time at Potter's warehouse."

"If you tell me where they play soldier, I'd like to find out what they used for targets tonight," Bolan stated.

Handler looked at the frightened faces of the survivors and gave the soldier directions to the militia's campsite twenty miles away.

"Give me a minute. I'm coming with you," he added.

"You're wounded, and you've got enough to do here."

Without a word, the sheriff walked to his vehicle, followed by Bolan.

Slipping into the driver's seat, Handler activated the small transceiver mounted beneath the dash and spelled out the situation to somebody on the other end.

"And you're going to need at least a dozen ambulances to take away the dead." He listened, then added, "I'll be back as soon as this man from Washington and I do a little snooping."

He pushed the off button and turned to Bolan. "State police. They'll get the ambulances up here."

He addressed the huddled group and explained that men and women were coming to take away the dead and find the rest housing for the night. Then he turned toward the Executioner to tell him he was going with him, but he had vanished.

Handler wondered where he had gone, then spotted the man carrying his canvas bag swiftly up the hill where the outlines of Army jeeps could be seen.

There was no way he could catch up to him. Instead, he waited for the state police and the ambulances.

CHAPTER NINE

Larry Potter was impatient. Marty Comer had promised the Carolina Militia chief that the truck would arrive just after midnight, filled with the weapons he had already sold to other groups. It was almost one, and the only sounds he heard were the loud chirping of birds.

The self-appointed colonel moved to where his men sat around a campfire. It was the right time to remind them why they were members of the Carolina Militia, and why they were waiting at the campsite. Potter knew he was a persuasive speaker. Sometimes even charismatic.

"Gather round," he ordered the seated men. The colonel proceeded to give the same lecture he had given for the past several years.

"Our country is being destroyed by the immigrants we let invade us on one pretext or another. And what do they bring with them? AIDS, other diseases and the need for us to support them. They contribute nothing beneficial, but like leeches, they suck our country dry.

"And who is responsible? The bleeding hearts in the government who want these creatures to become citizens so they can vote them into office again and again. Their stooges—the FBI, the DEA, the ATF and the U.S. Marshals—have murdered decent citizens because they happened to protest some illegal action of the government. And the people in Washington, D.C., help them cover up their crimes.

"We are going to stop these murders and bring the killers and the illegal immigrants back to justice—even if we have to carry out the sentence ourselves. That's why we're here. A new shipment of the latest weapons will be arriving any minute. As our ranks grow, we need more guns, more ammunition and more grenades. When the truck gets here, unload it into your pickup trucks and deliver it to the warehouse. I've got men waiting there to store them in a safe place so snooping federal agents can't find them."

Potter felt satisfied. He could tell his speech had impressed the men around the fire. Sometime later, he would tell them about the two young traitors he'd had to execute.

He stood and brushed the dirt and twigs from his combat pants. It was time to check that the perimeter guards were in place. They had been ordered to take care of their toilet needs before they took on guard duty.

He began to move along the outer rim of the campgrounds.

A gray-blond man, in a Carolina Militia uniform that was too big for him, snapped his assault rifle into an awkward salute when he saw Potter approach.

The colonel saluted back and stopped.

"Your name is Holbrook, isn't it?"

"Yes, sir. Steve Holbrook."

Potter had known the boy's family for years, solid Americans who owned a large farm south of Haywood. The old man had been killed in Korea, but his body was buried in a military graveyard in Asheville.

"This is your first mission for the militia?"

"Yes, Colonel." The fair-haired youth was anxious to impress his chief. "But I've been with the militia for three years."

"Good. How do you feel about these immigrants?"

The young man beamed and tightened his grip on the weapon in his hands.

"As far as I'm concerned, they should all be shipped back to Vietnam. They steal jobs from real Americans and take welfare money that ought to go to decent people. They're like blood-sucking leeches on a horse."

The Carolina Militia chief smiled at the young man. He was a perfect recruit for the organization. Like his father, he was proud of being an American and willing to die to keep the Feds from giving the country away to foreigners.

Potter started to move to the next guard, when he heard the loud sound of a truck coming closer.

"Pass the word to be alert until we get the truck unloaded and the crates into our pickups."

POTTER HAD ORDERED every militia member who owned a pickup truck to bring it with them that weekend. He didn't like having to carry so much cash—more than seventy thousand dollars—but he'd make much more than that when he resold the weapons. It was a profit of more than $275,000, and that wasn't counting what the ammo would bring.

He heard Holbrook yelling his orders to the guard, fifty yards from him.

The sentry, a man in his fifties, sporting a bushy mustache, acknowledged the orders and continued to yell the instructions to the next sentry on the perimeter.

Inside the guarded perimeter, men who had been lounging around the fire or quietly sharing cigarettes suddenly became busy. Weapons were returned to their holsters or slung back over a shoulder.

Johnny Skeeters, a tall man with a pronounced limp, dragged himself to Larry Potter's side. "Anything special you want, Colonel?"

"Yeah, Colonel. Have the men dismantle the tents," Potter ordered. "We've got a long drive ahead of us. I want to be ready to get on the road the minute the pickups are loaded."

Skeeters nodded and limped away to issue orders to his subordinates.

Within minutes, men started taking down the canvas shelters and carrying them to the trucks. Without waiting for orders, the men in the campsite area moved to where the truck was supposed to stop.

"Get the men ready to unload the truck," Potter shouted as he pushed through the waiting troops to look for Skeeters.

A brand-new Peterbilt 18-wheeler lumbered up to where the militia soldiers waited and stopped.

Behind the huge vehicle, sixteen bikers riding

Harley-Davidson motorcycles revved their engines in an ear-shattering salute, then shifted to neutral and cut the loud power plants.

Silence resumed as the passenger's door to the truck opened and a huge bearded man jumped to the ground. Wearing leather pants and a matching leather vest over his muscled bare chest, he looked at the several dozen uniformed men.

In a loud voice, he asked, "Who's Potter?"

The head of the Carolina Militia pushed through the crowd.

"I'm Colonel Potter."

The two men stared at each other in silence for more than a minute. Then the bearded man grinned and said, "I'm Lodge, and I've got some crates for you."

He signaled his men to open the back of the long truck. Turning to Sterno, Lodge said, "Have the guys move the boxes to the back platform. And don't forget those crates in the back are going someplace else."

Turning back to Potter, he commented, "So you're the head of this Carolina Militia our mutual friend has been telling me about."

"You'll be hearing a lot more about us in the next few days."

"Nothing good, I hope," Lodge said cynically.

"That's according to what side you're on," the militia chief retorted. "What side are you on?"

"Ever hear of the White Aryan Resistance?"

"I think I did. You the group that ran through that black area north of Jackson, Mississippi, firing guns at every black man you saw?"

"Yeah. And black women, too," Lodge bragged.

"Maybe we can team up sometime."

"Only if there's something in it for us." He looked at the crates being stacked on the truck platform. "Like now."

"I guess I better get my men started on moving those crates into our pickups."

"After you pay us," Lodge stated. "This is a cash-on-delivery deal."

"So our friend told me."

Potter reached down for the satchel. "I've got the amount our friend told me to bring," he said, handing the satchel.

Lodge handed the money to Sterno.

"Count how much is in there."

Then he faced Potter. "It's going to have to be a little more. We got hold of a couple of crates of some new AT 8 rockets and launchers. Knock out police cars, armored vans or even the side of a building."

"How much you looking for?"

Lodge thought for a moment. "Make it four grand. A real bargain at that price."

Potter had done business with other gangs like the WAR group, so he had carried an extra five thousand dollars inside his shirt.

"All I got on me is two thousand bucks."

"Make it three and we got a deal."

"Let me ask the men to take up a collection. Meanwhile, these men can start moving the crates. I'll be right back," Potter promised, and vanished through the crowds of militiamen.

Sliding into the front seat of his pickup truck, the surplus-military-goods dealer pulled the money out from inside his shirt, counted out three thousand dollars and hid the rest in his glove compartment.

Rejoining the head biker, he handed over the stack of hundred-dollar bills. Lodge quickly counted it.

"Pleasure doing business with you," the WAR leader commented.

"How about lending a hand getting the crates moved?" Potter asked.

Lodge thought about it. "That's not the deal." He called out orders to Sterno.

"The sooner we get the boxes transferred, the sooner we party."

Lodge countered with an offer to Potter. "How about joining us for some drinks? You can catch up with your boys later."

The militia head thought about it and grinned. He turned to Skeeters. "Colonel, get those pickups loaded and down to the warehouse. You know where to store them. I'll meet you there in the morning to check them out."

"Too bad we don't have some girls here," Potter commented.

Lodge winked. "Who said we didn't? Climb inside the truck, and we can start the party."

Potter was a customer, and Lodge remembered his daddy, a traveling salesman, telling him that a good salesman always treated his customers right so they would keep buying from him.

And this was a night Potter would remember.

BLENDING IN with the shadows, the blacksuited man moved swiftly to where the loaded pickup trucks were being parked. Bolan's face, covered with combat cosmetics, was expressionless. As he watched, the large truck and the bikers took off. He had arrived too late to stop them, but he could focus on the pickup trucks loaded with crates.

Bolan began his campaign in complete silence. Easily avoiding the handful of guards posted around the now dismantled compound, he hid and let a tall, uniformed figure pass. Intent on dumping the quickly folded tent he carried into one of the trucks, the militiaman didn't sense the presence of the armed intruder.

Sliding the razor-sharp combat blade from its sheath, Bolan slipped behind the uniformed sentry, spun him and rammed the blade under his ribs. Shoving the combat knife upward until he felt resistance from the man's heart muscle, he twisted the blade, then pulled it out and let the lifeless form sink to the ground.

He quickly pulled the tent and the body behind some bushes, then paused to tear the metal wolf's-head symbol from the dead man's collar and drop it into a pocket.

Looking around to make sure that no one had seen him, the Executioner propelled himself under the nearest truck.

Opening his canvas bag, he took out a block of C-4 plastique and attached it to the metal plate under the engine block. Checking the attached timer, he set it for forty-five minutes, which would give him enough time to complete the plan.

Working along the line of vehicles, the soldier attached plastique bombs to eight trucks.

Three blocks of explosive remained in the carryall, and the Executioner had a destination in mind for all of them.

The militiamen started to move toward their vehicles, and the Executioner knew he had to complete the first part of his mission swiftly. He crawled around a truck and crept to the seven jeeps, quickly cutting the three bricks in two. He was short of explosives for the last vehicle.

The soldier fixed the explosives to the engine blocks of six of the vehicles, and started to pop the hood so he could tear out the distributor wires. But the sounds of footsteps behind him were nearing rapidly.

Bolan sprinted across the campsite, heading for the military-surplus jeep he'd appropriated, which was parked several hundred yards from the compound.

"Hey, you," a voice shouted. "What you doing there?"

Bolan zigzagged into a broken-field trot, shifting the Uzi from his shoulder to his hands as he ran. He squeezed the trigger and hosed the shouting man with 9 mm Parabellum rounds before the guy could unleash the deadly power of his Colt assault rifle.

The corpse collapsed to the ground, watering the dust with blood.

A group of militiamen raced from the parking area, aiming M-16s in the direction of the gunfire. A hail of concentrated slugs tore into the air where Bolan had been a moment earlier.

He'd dropped to the ground, still grasping his carryall. A series of side rolls carried him several yards from where the body had fallen.

A flaxen-haired young man hungry for glory raced toward him, wildly firing his Colt rifle. Feeling sad about the life the young man would never have, Bolan fired a burst into the youth's chest.

The Executioner hurried through the wooded area as stealthily as possible. He could hear men yelling and cursing as they crashed through the brush in search of him. He replaced his empty clip and fired a 3-round burst at the sudden movement of a bush. A uniformed body fell on top of the thorns.

Stomping footfalls behind a stand of trees alerted the soldier. He pulled a frag grenade from his combat vest, pulled the pin and tossed the bomb in their direction.

Several bodies were catapulted into the air by the force of the detonation. Survivors lay moaning in the dark.

There was no way Bolan could make it back to his vehicle on foot. Then he spotted the outlines of the trucks and jeeps he had rigged to blow up. He took a chance and sprinted for the jeep he hadn't touched. Glancing at the steering column, he saw that the keys were still in the ignition.

Tossing another grenade into the woods to slow his pursuers, Bolan jumped into the driver's seat, cranked the engine to life and tore down the dirt road to where he had parked the other confiscated jeep.

In the distance, he heard a voice shout, "In the trucks. After him. Don't let him get away!"

The jeep was still there. He rocked the military vehicle to a stop and tossed the key into the thick brush. In seconds flat, he was out of one jeep and into another.

As he drove away, the soldier checked his watch. The time had come. He stopped the vehicle and covered his ears with his hands as a series of violent explosions pierced the night. For a brief moment, the skies lit up with the intensity of a fireworks display.

Having to kill the young man saddened Bolan,

but no matter his age, he had made a choice. The youth was a casualty of war. There would be many others before peace came to this corner of North Carolina.

He had one in mind as he drove away.

CHAPTER TEN

Chief Deputy Sheriff Billy Tom Perkins had been sent by Sheriff Rusher to make sure Lodge was satisfied with the price for the weapons the Carolina Militia didn't buy. He knew Sheriff Rusher was expecting him to come back with the weapons in his van, and he was worried about disappointing him.

A disappointed Jeff Rusher was someone Perkins didn't want to have to face. The sheriff was short and stout. His hair was gray and he was past sixty, but Perkins had seen him whip out a revolver and kill two men in seconds.

Rusher might be old, but he also was mean.

He had seen how the sheriff reacted to disappointment in the past. Such as when Tom Miller, one of his closest friends, had announced he made all the money he needed and was quitting. Rusher got that too sweet smile on his face, patted old

Tom on the back and wished him luck. Nobody ever saw Tom Miller after that. He had vanished suddenly, like a jug of corn whiskey at a country party.

Perkins didn't want to disappear like Miller.

Rusher had a good thing going—buying guns from hijackers and storing them until they found a buyer who was willing to pay ten to twenty times what the sheriff had paid for the weapons. And he always cut in Perkins and the others for a share—as a sign of appreciation for their help.

The best thing about Rusher's business was that there were no cops to bother them. Perkins laughed at his private joke. Sheriff Jeff Rusher was the law.

The meeting was supposed to take place where the Carolina Militia held their training sessions, but all Perkins could find were the hulks of burned-out trucks, and bodies shattered by the huge explosion he had heard while driving to the site.

He swung his truck around and headed back to the sheriff's office.

LODGE HAD RACED to Rusher's office when he saw the pickups start to explode through the rear-view mirror, and he watched through a window as a police car pulled up to the curb. He signaled his men, who grabbed their automatic weapons and eyeballed the deputy as he walked into the sheriff's office.

Nervously, Perkins mumbled an apology for getting to the Carolina Militia's training grounds too late, then looked stunned when he saw Lodge.

"I saw...the bodies," he stuttered.

"Not ours," Lodge replied casually and turned to the sheriff.

"Where do we unload your shipment?"

"I got a farm six miles from here. We'll put the crates in the shed there." He drew a crude road map and handed it over.

Lodge took it and turned to Sterno. "What about Potter?"

"I left the little blonde with him at the motel when I checked us in. She'll keep him from thinking about anything else all night." He checked his wristwatch. "We should be back at the motel in a few hours." He grinned. "Then we can start *our* party."

"I've got some business to take care of," Rusher said. "Front door's open. Meet you there in fifteen minutes."

Nodding, Lodge and his men took off.

The sheriff turned to Perkins. "You stay here in case somebody shows up with a problem."

The deputy looked nervous. "Me? What if they're looking for you or Lodge?"

Rusher opened a weapons locker, which was filled with automatic weapons.

"That's what these are here for," he reminded the frightened deputy. "And call me on the car radio."

RUSHER STARTED to walk toward the farmhouse, but remembered something. He returned to the trunk of his car and took out an aluminum attaché case and a stubby 9 mm Uzi machine pistol. He checked the side arms the deputies who were with him wore in their leather holsters. "Everyone got their guns on cock-and-lock?"

The three men nodded. The sheriff jacked a round into the firing chamber of his weapon and led the way up the broken slate path that led to the front door.

As they approached the door, Rusher whispered his final instructions to one of his men. Showing no reaction, the man nodded.

RUSHER AND LODGE STOOD inside a circle of gang members and deputies, discussing the price for the shipment.

The sheriff studied the gang leader's face. "How many pieces you got?"

"We double-checked after we got here. We got about six hundred M-16s and sixty cases of ammo."

Rusher held out his hand. "We got a deal."

"At the price we talked about over the phone," Lodge reminded him.

"Sure," the sheriff replied, smiling.

The two men shook hands.

"Let's get the stuff loaded into my shed," Rusher said, tapping the aluminum case. "Then you get this."

"Let's see what you got inside," Lodge said, his voice filled with suspicion.

Rusher opened the case, which was filled with stacks of neatly wrapped hundred-dollar bills.

For almost an hour, the bikers and Rusher's men worked as a team, lugging case after case out of the truck and moving them into the shed behind the sheriff's isolated farmhouse.

Lodge and the sheriff stood to one side, watching the teams of men sweating as they made the transfer. Rusher held his Uzi in one hand.

"Why the hell don't you put that away? Makes me nervous," Lodge said, sounding annoyed.

"Just in case somebody who shouldn't be here shows up. Where's your piece?"

The head biker lifted his black T-shirt to reveal a massive .357-caliber Desert Eagle pistol.

"Reliable gun," the lawman said approvingly.

"We picked them up in that raid six months ago. The one on that importer's warehouse."

The sheriff remembered. He'd purchased part of the inventory of guns and ammunition for resale to his clients.

Rusher was getting impatient with the time it was taking to transfer the merchandise. "How close are we to being finished?"

Lodge walked over to the truck the White Aryan Resistance bikers had stolen and peered inside. "Almost done," he announced.

"After we're loaded up, let's drive your truck down the road a few miles and torch it," Rusher suggested. "Make it harder for anybody to figure out what happened."

"Good idea. There's a barrel of kerosene inside we could use."

The gang leader addressed his men. "Let's get a move on. We've got a big party to get started at the motel," he announced, "and the bread to pay for it."

"Don't forget to pull your bikes down the

driveway, away from the shed,'' the lawman suggested.

The bike gang saw Poker standing on the rear end of the truck. ''Get some of the guys busy moving our bikes closer to the road, so we can blow this pop stand.''

Poker looked around, then spied the women standing nearby. ''Hey, you bitches start earning your keep. Get the hogs moved.''

Struggling with the heavyweight motorcycles, the women wheeled them slowly down the dirt road. One of the bikes toppled over as a small bleached blonde tried to roll it back on its kickstand.

''One more dumb move like that,'' Poker yelled, ''and you walk all the way home!''

The blonde quickly righted the bike, grunting with the weight as she did.

Poker checked the inside of the truck. ''Everything's been moved,'' he told the sheriff.

He jumped down from the rear end of the truck and walked over to where Lodge and the sheriff stood. He looked at the gang chief. ''What next?''

''We settle up.''

''First I get one of my men to help you move the truck down the road,'' Rusher replied.

The biker stared at the lawman coldly. "No. First you pay."

Rusher looked down the driveway at the men walking toward him. It was all falling into place, just the way he knew it would. They'd have more than enough time to get ready for the buyer.

He made a quick decision. He'd pay Lodge now, then retrieve the money after the bikers were dead. He opened the trunk of his official car and took the case.

"What did it come to?" he asked. "Twelve thousand, five hundred?"

"Fifteen thousand, five hundred," Lodge replied icily.

Rusher nodded and counted out the bundled stacks of hundred-dollar bills, smiling at the biker. "I think you'll find it all there," he said pleasantly, gripping the trigger of the Uzi submachine gun he held against his leg.

He waited for the right moment. It never came.

Lodge smiled coldly at the lawman.

"I hate cops who try to cheat me," the head biker said, firing three metal-jacketed rounds into the sheriff's surprised face.

Rusher's deputies ran toward the bikers, yanking their handguns from their waistband holsters. Lodge's men had expected their move.

Drawing Tec-9s and Ingram subguns from under their heavy leather jackets, they emptied their clips at Rusher's men.

Sterno and Poker returned to Lodge, nodding at the bike gang leader.

"I'll take the money now," Lodge said, reaching for the case the sheriff had leaned on the trunk of the car.

Rusher stirred on the ground and gasped a question. "Why?"

"You became a liability when you decided to try to cheat me," the head biker explained patiently, and fired several rounds of burning lead into Rusher's face.

He turned away and looked down the driveway. "You all finished down there?" he called out.

"We checked each of them," one of his men shouted back. "They're dead."

The biker chief was pleased. "Got some matches?"

"Yeah, sure," one of the other men said. "Why?"

The biker chief turned to Sterno. "You find that can of kerosene in the back of the truck?"

"Yeah. I wetted down the sheriff's place like you told me."

"Torch the house," Lodge ordered, then

reached into his pocket and took out a book of matches. He looked at the words on the cover: Sparky's Home Cooking. He remembered the place. Run-down looking, but some of the best country cooking in the state. He reminded himself that he should drop in the next time he had to be in western North Carolina on business.

He moved back from the barn and struck a match. The match head sputtered, then burst into flame. Lodge stared at it, hypnotized for a moment, then tossed it at the dark, pungent-smelling pool on the ground in front of the door.

The kerosene burst into a river of fire, moving rapidly toward the wooden structure. Lodge threw the book of matches to the ground and hurried down the driveway to where the bikes were parked.

Behind him, he heard a rumbling explosion as the flames came in contact with the police car's gasoline tank. To his right, he could feel the heat of the burning farmhouse. He turned and saw Poker running down the pathway.

As quickly as he could move his stocky body, the biker boss joined his men as they watched the flames light up the sky.

"Take some of the other men and hightail it back to the shed," he said to Sterno. "Start moving the cases back into the truck."

CHAPTER ELEVEN

Bolan contacted Sheriff Handler at his office and suggested that they pay a call to Sheriff Rusher. According to Handler, Rusher was a small-time gun supplier, but it was possible that he knew who was supplying the Carolina Militia.

A deputy behind a desk looked up as the two men entered the front office. He smiled when he saw one of them was Handler. A second deputy, sitting at a nearby table, thumbing through a girlie magazine, didn't stir.

Handler led the conversation. "Sheriff Rusher around?"

"He'll be back in a couple of hours, Sheriff."

"We need to find him now. Where is he?"

"Out on business."

"Law enforcement or personal?"

Perkins could feel the hostility from Handler

and the man with him. He'd better warn his boss that something was up.

"Would you excuse me? I'll be right back."

He got up and started to walk to the back door. Bolan moved quickly and stood between Perkins and the exit.

"Going somewhere?"

"The...the bathroom," the deputy mumbled.

The soldier stepped aside and let the lawman open the door.

Perkins raced for the back of the sheriff's office. Then, as he got to the lot behind the building, he remembered his truck was parked in front. He noticed Molly Carson coming out of the small grocery store next door toting several bags. Her teenage daughter, Lori, was similarly burdened with groceries. The older woman struggled to push her key into her van door.

"Let me help you, Ms. Carson," the deputy said, grabbing the keys from her hand.

"No need. We can manage."

Perkins shoved her to the ground as he tore the driver's door open.

"What are you doing?" the woman yelled. "You're stealing my car. Stop!"

The deputy pulled the 9 mm Smith & Wesson 459 pistol from his waistband holster and pumped lead into the screaming woman to silence her. The second uniformed deputy burst out of the back door of the office and forced the teenager into the van. He ordered Perkins to drive it out of the back lot and onto the street.

BOLAN COULD HEAR the hysterical screams of a young girl from inside the van. The soldier charged the twenty feet that separated him from the van, reached under the back of his jacket and grabbed the 9 mm Beretta from its shoulder holster.

Assuming a two-handed combat stance, Bolan fired a 3-round burst at the fleeing vehicle.

The rounds sheared the tips of Perkins's fingers from his gun hand, and the pistol fell from his numb hand.

The driver shoved a Smith & Wesson pistol out of the open window, closed a finger against the trigger and drilled a pair of shots at Bolan.

Someone behind the Executioner fired two scorching rounds that cored into Perkins's face, disintegrating the man's features into a mass of frothing blood and bone splinters. What was left of his head slumped out of sight in the cab of the van as the automatic weapon clattered to the roadway.

The crowd moved farther from the vehicle as they saw the sheriff and the man with him shooting at the pair of killers.

The remaining gunman suddenly panicked. He shoved Perkins's body out the driver's door and dragged the girl to his side.

"Let her go," Handler yelled, as the Executioner moved closer to the curb.

The frightened killer hugged the hysterical girl closer. "I'll blow her away if you don't get out of here!" he threatened.

Handler muttered a curse as they heard the deputy shout at her to drive.

The van continued on as the deputy leaned out his window and showered the area with 9 mm Parabellum slugs.

Handler and Bolan scattered to avoid the ricocheting lead. When the sheriff had a chance to look for Bolan, he saw him leaning against a No Parking stanchion, blood seeping from a wound on his cheek.

"You okay?" he asked.

The hard-faced warrior was too busy scanning the area to reply. He raced to a nearby car, whose driver hastily exited the vehicle, realizing Bolan's intent.

The sheriff sensed the soldier's goal and

sprinted after him, rolling himself across the front hood to get to the other side as Bolan started the engine. Yanking the front passenger's door open, Handler hauled himself inside as Bolan threw the vehicle into gear and stomped on the gas pedal.

THE STOLEN VAN slowed at a crossroad, then made a hard right.

Lori became hysterical and started to pummel the deputy with her fists.

With one hand on the wheel, the deputy raised his pistol, aimed it at her face and fired twice.

The force of the rounds drove her against the passenger's door.

The uniformed thug didn't have time to open the door and shove out the body, not with the chase vehicle so close behind.

He took another right and raced down the road, heading toward Sheriff Rusher's farm. There would be enough of Rusher's men there to take care of the pair chasing him.

He forced the gas pedal to the floor and skidded along the pavement.

SUDDENLY, THE VAN was ahead of them. Bolan set his jaw and floored the gas pedal.

"Not good," he said angrily.

Handler understood. There could be only one explanation for the explosions they had heard seconds earlier.

"She's dead," the sheriff said bluntly.

"So's he," the Executioner replied.

Buffeted by the air pressure its high speed was creating, the van swerved back and forth across the road. Suddenly, the vehicle careened onto a side road.

"He's heading for the Cherokee reservation," Bolan said, after reading a small sign on the side of the road. "We'll take him there."

"Not the reservation," Handler snapped. "Rusher's farm is four or five miles down this road. What do you want to do?"

"Stop him, one way or the other."

"I'm with you," Handler growled.

The soldier pressed harder on the gas pedal and began to inch up on the van.

Spinning almost out of control at the curves, the van tried to pull away. Bolan kept up the pressure, edging the borrowed car closer to the other vehicle as he inched forward.

Wrenching the wheel, Bolan rammed his right fender against the rear quarter of the van. He then turned away from the van, spun the steering wheel and ran a diagonal line at the front of the other vehicle.

They could see the panicked deputy's face as he tried to avoid being hit.

The deep, narrow ditch on his left rushed up to grab his left tires. Terrified, he spun the wheel, trying desperately to gain the roadway.

A farmhouse loomed several hundred yards ahead, flames reaching up to the sky.

"Rusher's place," Handler snapped. "Someone hit it hard."

The deputy raced the van up the driveway. At high speed, he had no time to stop before colliding with the sheriff's car parked directly in front of him. Suddenly, it was too late. The collision forced the van to roll over on its side.

Bolan slowed the car and stopped next to the overturned vehicle. He could detect no movement from inside.

Sheriff Handler looked at his temporary partner. "Think he's dead?"

Bolan shoved a fresh clip into his Beretta and opened his door. "Let's check it out."

The two men eased out of the vehicle and separated as they approached the van. They stood a short distance away and listened intently.

Carefully, they moved to the passenger's door.

As the Executioner kept his finger against the trigger of the silenced 93-R, the sheriff twisted the handle and pulled it open.

The young deputy was crushed against the steering wheel, jammed into a corner by the bleeding body of the innocent young woman.

He forced his lids open and stared at the two men. "I'm hurting, you bastard."

"Suffer," Handler said, slamming the door.

CHAPTER TWELVE

The dirt around the destroyed farmhouse was covered with motorcycle tracks and dead bodies.

Handler looked at Bolan. "Any suspects?"

"One. The White Aryan Resistance."

The sheriff nodded his agreement, then studied the bloody bodies. Rusher's corpse was torn almost beyond recognition.

"Couldn't have happened to a more deserving guy," Handler commented.

"I saw a gang of bikers hightailing it from the woods when I took on Potter's men," Bolan observed. "I wondered where they were heading."

In response, the sheriff used his car radio to contact the local state police barracks.

"Any word of a large gathering of bikers around these parts?" he asked, then listened. "Thanks. What was the name of that motel?"

He listened, then turned to Bolan. "The High Top, in Lexington. A fleabag."

"How long will it take for us to get there?"

"An hour if we rush."

Bolan gave the problem some thought.

"Where would they go if they left there?" he mused. He looked at the sheriff. "Would they go to Potter's warehouse?" Bolan remembered the large truck that sped away from the mountain training site.

"I don't know," Handler admitted. "Why would they?"

"In addition to being a bigot, Potter's a gun dealer. He wouldn't just vanish and leave his inventory."

"It's worth finding out," the sheriff agreed.

THE HEAD OF THE Carolina Militia woke up with a pounding headache. The young hooker lying in bed next to him smiled as she slipped out from under the covers and started to put on her clothes. Potter recognized her as the blonde who had been sitting in the back of Lodge's truck.

"You ain't bad for an old man," she said as she looked into a wall mirror and smeared some bright red lipstick on her lips.

Potter didn't remember taking her to his room.

The last thing he could recall was driving up to a run-down motel just outside of town in Lodge's truck.

And the amount of liquor he started to consume.

Everything else was a blank. He hoped his troops didn't see him take off with the bikers. Discipline had to be maintained in order to keep his men in line.

The woman pulled a skintight T-shirt over her head, then stepped into a miniskirt and hooked it closed.

"Nice meeting you," she said as she opened the room door and stepped outside.

Larry Potter wasn't sure where he was, or how to get back to his house or warehouse. That was the least of his problems. Right now, he needed some aspirin to kill the agony inside his head.

The door swung open and Lodge entered, carrying a bottle.

"I think you need a drink, buddy," the head biker said, waving the bottle and a water glass.

"It's the last thing I need," Potter groaned.

"You better take a shot anyway before I break the news to you," the biker stated as he filled the glass with whiskey and handed it across the bed.

The Carolina Militia leader took the glass from

Lodge's hand, intending to set it on the night-stand.

The biker walked across the room and turned on the television set.

"You better watch this."

A newscaster was talking about finding the Montagnard bodies at a farm on the edge of the Great Smoky Mountains Park.

"More than thirty men, women and children were found slain. In addition, the bodies of eighteen men were found. All were wearing emblems indicating they were members of the Carolina Militia, a local organization that has long fought to have the Southeast Asian refugees sent back to Vietnam. Sheriff Doug Handler, head of the Haywood County Sheriff's Department, claimed that he had found the men killing the refugees..."

Potter crawled out of bed and turned off the set.

He looked concerned. "Any comment about them looking for me?"

Lodge smiled. "Don't get your bowels in an uproar. Not a word about a manhunt for the 'colonel.'" He laughed. "They're not even sure who killed them people at the farm."

"Really?"

"Every time some of my guys take off on

somebody, the cops haul me in for questioning because I've done a lot of talking out loud about how whites are better than anybody else. My mouthpiece just keeps yelling that they're violating my First Amendment rights."

"So does Andy Sturgis," Potter admitted reluctantly.

"Who's this Sturgis?"

"My lawyer."

"Just tell them you didn't send the men or order them to kill anybody."

Potter grabbed the drink on the nightstand and swallowed a mouthful. The taste made him gag.

"What you gotta worry about more," Lodge continued, "is who blew up all the pickup trucks and jeeps at your campsite."

Potter looked stunned. "What?"

"It's all over the news. All those weapons and ammo we delivered went up like a Fourth of July display according to the news broadcast. They're guessing fifty or more men were killed in the explosion."

"Do they blame the Carolina Militia?"

Lodge shrugged. "Not yet. After they got all the fires out, there wasn't enough left of anything to identify the bodies. All the local sheriff would say was that he was still investigating." He shook his head as he studied the look of horror on Potter's face. "They will eventually when they check the serial numbers on the trucks. But you just keep denying you had anything to do with anything except helping those guys' complaints against the government be heard."

The surplus dealer suddenly felt trapped. He had lost more than seventy thousand dollars and a lot of men. Men could be replaced, but the money?

"Just came to tell you that we're pulling out of here. And you should do the same—at least for a while."

"Can you give me a lift to my warehouse?"

"Sure," Lodge said, "if you move your ass. Meet you outside."

"How about going partners?" Potter asked cautiously.

The head biker looked surprised. "What'd you have in mind?"

"We use your truck to move some special inventory I've got in my warehouse. I might be able to find somebody who'll buy it right away." He could see the look of skepticism in Lodge's face. "I've got lots of connections."

Larry Potter knew he had a lot of calls to make.

First call would be to his lawyer, then he'd call Marty Comer.

Comer should be able to tell him what to do. The broadcaster was always getting himself out of trouble.

LARRY POTTER'S WAREHOUSE sold all kinds of surplus military goods to customers, including used weapons to people who were qualified to buy them. He even had a small outdoor range behind the shop that faced the town dump.

But Potter was best known as a general surplus dealer. Scattered on the rest of the lot were all kinds of surplus: used military trucks, vans and cars; vintage World War II tanks that didn't work but were sought after by war buffs and film studios looking for cheap equipment they could use in war movies; overstocks from manufacturers of everything from overalls to farm equipment.

There wasn't much Potter wasn't willing to offer good, hard cash for, especially from the military. Tents, uniforms, paratrooper boots, field cooking gear—the list was endless.

Larry Potter tended to wear old clothes. It was part of the image he wanted to present to customers. He was a wealthy man, but he didn't believe in displaying it. He could demand higher prices if his customers thought he was having a hard time making ends meet.

The yard of his warehouse, surrounded by an electrified wire fence, was filled with the larger items of his surplus inventory.

Inside, Potter stored his more valuable inventory. Large stocks of television sets and personal computers acquired at bankruptcy auctions, cases of auto parts and a hundred other categories were stacked in tall rows set far enough apart to allow a forklift to move between them.

There was a separate area for stacks of literature: copies of racist magazines and newspapers, reprints of bigot tracts and books on how to effectively use violence to fight the government.

Potter had a ready-made audience for the literature. Members of the Carolina Militia were required to buy and read the magazines, newspapers and books. And thanks to the publicity he regularly received from Marty Comer, the controversial talk-radio host, each week he received dozens of orders from every corner of the country.

Comer was one of several hundred broadcasters who made money feeding fuel to the racist hate fires that burned throughout the country. Not all of them appealed to white supremacist audiences.

There were those who fed on the resentment and fury of blacks and other nonwhite groups.

And unlike Comer, not all of them survived on payoffs from the racist groups to whom they appealed. For most, there were enough advertisers to make their messages of hate and revenge profitable.

Larry Potter, for example, paid Comer for the daily publicity he received. Even for someone as tightfisted as the surplus dealer, the money he gave the broadcaster had paid off tenfold in sales of literature.

But even more important, Comer was his link to powerful men in government who passed on information and tips to the broadcaster. In turn, Comer passed on the information to people like Larry Potter.

The surplus dealer was certain that Comer had other groups to whom he gave the same information. But that didn't matter to Potter, as long as he was forewarned about problems and opportunities.

Like the mercenary who had attacked the campsite.

The newspapers and television stations were filled with news of the death of thirty-five of the Vietnamese, and claimed the dead soldiers the police found at the farm and at the campsite were responsible.

The head of the Carolina Militia sat at his paper-cluttered desk and stared into space. He had barely escaped being one of the dead when the pickup trucks and jeeps exploded.

The safe in the floor under his desk was already empty. Its contents were stored in four canvas duffel bags. Membership records and other files of the Carolina Militia were burning in the old-fashioned woodstove that heated the concrete block structure in the winter.

The thing that bothered him was that Lodge was watching his every move. The biker sat in a chair and stared at him. Even when he got his cash out of the safe.

"Looks like you had a pretty good business here," Lodge commented.

Potter didn't know how to answer, so he remained silent as he went about his business. He had left a detailed message for Marty Comer at his studio, and Andy Sturgis said he'd handle the local authorities.

As Lodge's men prepared to move his inventory from behind the false wall to their truck, the phone rang.

It was Marty Comer.

Quickly, Potter told him what had happened, putting emphasis on how somebody—probably federal agents—had murdered seventy or more members of the Carolina Militia.

"Hang tight, Larry. Call me in an hour. I have to talk to some people."

CHAPTER THIRTEEN

Outside the surplus junkyard, Bolan and Sheriff Handler pulled up in the sheriff's vehicle and cautiously worked their way down the packed dirt road to the tall fence that surrounded Potter's place. The gates to the yard were locked.

A large hand-painted sign hung on the inside of the fence. Potter's Surplus Warehouse Closed Today it announced. There were no guards visible, only row after row of surplus equipment, and the tall, mesh-wire fence that prevented vandals from breaking in and stealing it.

The soldier had called Handler early in the morning to get a status report on the Montagnard and campsite survivors. The two had met for coffee at a small diner outside of town.

"The press has been on my ass for more information, but I kept your name out of it," Handler had reported.

"You could have," Bolan replied. "I'm used to taking the heat."

"Only problem was that I couldn't convince Judge Wickers to issue a search warrant of Potter's home and warehouse. Potter and he have been members of the same lodge for twenty years."

Bolan had run into the same situation too many times to be surprised, bleeding-heart judges who refused to believe that their social friends were anything but perfect.

"I don't need a warrant," Bolan stated. "You do."

"The warehouse isn't in my jurisdiction," the sheriff reminded Bolan as he reached for the badge pinned to his shirt and took it off. "Now, neither do I."

Bolan studied the sheriff's expressionless face. "Why?"

"I can't get the picture of all the murdered men, women and kids out of my head."

The Executioner weighed the self-extended invitation, then made a decision.

"Okay. But you're on your own. And you follow orders."

TWO BEARDED, leather-clad men exited one of the warehouse's wide doors, complaining to each other in low voices. Each carried a 9 mm MAC-10 slung across a shoulder.

"Guards?" the sheriff asked quietly. He and Bolan watched from some bushes as the men scanned the area.

"They look more like bikers than warehouse workers," the soldier commented. Bolan was ready for combat. His silenced 9 mm Beretta was tucked into its shoulder holster, while the .44 Magnum Desert Eagle rode in leather at his hip. The Applegate-Fairbairn knife was locked to his wrist by its rigid sheath.

The grenades he had yanked from the combat vest he wore had been replaced, as had the C-4 plastic explosives, detonators and timers.

The Uzi submachine gun was slung over a shoulder. Replacement magazines for it and the two handguns were tucked in vest pockets.

Doug Handler had come prepared. Across his right shoulder was an AR-15, chambered to handle 5.56 mm rounds, and in the holster hanging from his heavy leather belt was his Colt Python revolver. Bulges in his jacket pockets revealed where he had stored extra magazines for the assault rifle and quick-loads for the Python.

Bolan had glanced at the weapons when they

had gotten out of Handler's van. At least the lawman wasn't depending solely on his Colt revolver.

He turned his attention to the men who had just entered the yard. One of the men raised his voice. "I don't give a shit what Lodge says. I'm not risking my neck for the leader of a bunch of play soldiers."

The other man looked annoyed. "Keep it down. If Lodge hears you, Poker takes you for a final hike."

The first man sounded skeptical. "Yeah, but you heard the news today. Cops are going to be swarming all over this place in a couple of hours. If they find me with guns, they got me on violating my parole."

"I wonder why those weekend wonders decided to eighty-six the Commies?"

The two men glanced around, then turned and went back into the warehouse.

Bolan looked at the lawman's right hand, gripping and ungripping the Colt Python in his holster. He could feel the anger flowing from every pore in Handler's body.

The Executioner understood. All of them had suffered painful personal losses, but the commitment he had made—at least to himself—was not to spend more than a few moments living in the sorrow. As much as the sheriff cared about the Southeast Asian refugees, he would have to learn that lesson in order to survive.

Without a word, Handler slipped the revolver from its rigid leather holder and moved closer to the high fence. He found a remnant of metal on the ground and tossed it at the barrier wires. There were no sparks.

"They must have forgotten to turn on the power to the fence," the local lawman whispered.

"Cover me," Bolan whispered back, and began to climb over the barrier. He dropped to the ground and waited for Handler to follow.

The sheriff climbed to the top of the fence, let the AR-15 drop into the soldier's waiting hands and let himself fall.

Bolan handed the assault weapon back to him, then knelt and unsheathed the wedge-shaped carbon-steel combat knife strapped to his left arm.

Leading the way, he slipped behind a huge, obsolete Caterpillar earthmover sitting by itself in a corner of the junk-filled yard and crouched. Handler copied him.

The two guards came out of the warehouse again and looked around.

"Lodge is getting paranoid about being attacked since last night," one of them said, sniggering. The other biker looked around nervously to make sure nobody heard the comment.

BOLAN SIGNALED Handler to follow his lead. He grabbed the nearer gunmen around the neck and slid the razor-sharp blade across his prey's throat from ear to ear, creating a crimson-colored smile.

The biker turned and stared at him in shock for a moment, then crumpled in a heap on the ground as life pumped out of both arteries.

The second biker swung his MAC-10 toward the sheriff.

"No way, José," Handler said in quiet anger as he quickly stood and chopped at the man's throat with the edge of his palm.

The peculiar sound of bones breaking in the neck could be heard as his palm pushed through them and ruptured the guard's carotid artery. The once sniggering man spun and fell against the side of the huge construction vehicle, then slid slowly into the dirt.

The two men stopped and listened for any sounds that might indicate their attack had been heard. There was none. Instead, the yard was filled with an eerie silence.

"Where'd you learn to do that?" Bolan asked softly.

"Special Forces. Fort Bragg. I used to be an instructor," came the reply.

Bolan studied the lawman's face. Some of the anger was gone, vented on the form on the ground. The soldier led the way to the warehouse doors in a half crouch. The lawman was right behind him, moving fast to catch up.

The soldier pulled him against the warehouse wall the moment he glanced up and spotted the surly-looking man standing at the edge of the roof. He was leaning over a huge unipod mounted weapon, which the Executioner recognized as a .50-caliber Barrett light machine gun.

With a muzzle velocity of 2800 feet per second, the weapon was one of the largest available that didn't require vehicle transport or a crew to operate it. The Barrett fired the largest-caliber ammunition available—the .50-caliber Browning cartridge—but, like anything else, the weapon was only as good as the person firing it. And the man on the roof wasn't sure when he should start firing.

The Executioner had no such problem. He pointed his silenced Uzi at the roof and unleashed two rounds with deadly accuracy. The dead biker toppled from the edge of the roof to the junk-filled yard.

The muffled explosions from the Israeli sub-machine gun were still audible, at least to Bolan and the sheriff, and they wondered if anybody else had heard them, too.

The two men waited to see if anyone came out of the warehouse.

Nobody did.

They peered inside. Other than the tall stacks of surplus merchandise lined up in rows, there was nothing and no one in the building. It was as if the rest of the rats had run out on the three dead men outside.

Neither of the invaders was fooled. Attempts to lull each of them into similar traps had been unsuccessfully tried before. The piles of cartons were adequate hiding places for assassins. Behind any of the stacks, one or more armed killers could be waiting for them to pass by.

They moved cautiously into the building, trying to make as little noise as possible, but the open space exaggerated the sounds of their movement.

''I wonder where Larry Potter is hiding?'' Handler whispered.

Before Bolan could answer, they both heard a shuffling noise from above them. Glancing up, they spotted two men carrying Tec-9s climb over the top of a stack of cartons from the other side.

Before Bolan or Handler could respond, the men had dropped on their stomachs and pointed their automatic weapons at the pair.

There was no time to aim. The Executioner and Handler swung their weapons into play, squeezing off bursts that drilled into their targets and blew them off their feet.

They didn't stop to admire their handiwork, as they could hear the movement of booted feet rushing toward them from the other end of the warehouse.

Bolan reached for the 40 mm fragmentation grenade on his belt, pulled the pin and threw the multigrooved weapon in a slow looping spin over the tops of the tall stacks.

"Duck!" the soldier yelled as the grenade exploded into thousands of deadly metal fragments across the wide room.

The two invaders could hear the screams of dying men from behind the far cartons as a small fire started inside a large cardboard box.

Crouching behind some cartons, they waited to see how many men would attack.

"Let's get rid of them now!" someone shouted.

Bolan replaced his almost empty clip with a

fresh magazine and stood, the Uzi set to continuous fire.

Nine men charged; nine men died.

Not quite nine yet, the soldier decided as he heard the moaning from one of them. He advanced and leaned over the blood-covered dying man.

"Where's Potter?" Bolan asked.

"Gone," the man gasped, then moaned in pain. "God it hurts."

"You'll be okay," Handler lied. "Where did Potter go?"

"Meeting Comer," the man replied, forcing out the words with great effort.

"What was he driving?" the sheriff prodded.

"Truck. Moving truck," the dying man mumbled. "We're...meeting him...later." With those words, the man breathed his last breath.

LIKE DOZENS of other highly verbal hate peddlers, Marty Comer, a former CIA agent, syndicated his two-hour talk show to stations around the United States. His continued advocacy of fighting agents of the federal government—and his demands that refugees be shipped back to their countries of origin—had created a climate of violent reaction among hate groups.

Efforts had been made by federal and state officials to stop Comer from preaching his message of hate and violence, but his pair of attorneys, Andy Sturgis and Gary Baling, had successfully argued that such actions would violate the broadcaster's right to free speech, guaranteed under the Constitution.

The two lawyers not only got paid handsomely for their legal efforts, but they also believed in what Comer preached. Both were active leaders in white-supremacist movements.

The short bald man held the telephone away from his ear. Larry Potter was shouting into it.

"What am I supposed to do if the Feds try to arrest me?" Potter yelled.

Comer took a deep breath to calm himself.

"Relax, Larry. And listen to my broadcast today. After I'm done, you'll be an American hero and the goddamned Feds will sound like a bunch of Nazi gestapo troopers trying to crucify you. I might even be able to get Grant Lightfoot to talk about you."

Lightfoot was the most famous of the racist broadcasters. A former White House aide, the ex-FBI agent kept preaching that the only good federal agent was a dead federal agent.

His words found sympathetic ears around the

country. And, despite his insistence that he was only voicing his opinion as guaranteed by the American Constitution, his paranoid preaching caused a number of psychopaths to attempt to assassinate FBI, ATF and IRS agents.

At the mention of Grant Lightfoot's name, Potter sounded less frantic.

"Well, some of them killed some of Lodge's people at the warehouse trying to get to me," he reported. "But I beat them. While they were killing his men, Lodge helped me load my special inventory into a truck and get away."

Potter's "special" inventory contained enough heavy-duty weapons to equip a small army.

Comer lowered his voice. "Where is it now? I've got people who want it."

"Parked outside this coffee shop I'm at. Got any ideas where I can store it?"

The broadcaster put the phone on his desk and pondered the question. One of his sponsors might be willing to buy Potter's weapons and ammo— if the surplus dealer offered them at a good price.

He pursued the thought with Potter.

"There's a group whose leader is down in Alabama. He mentioned he needed more weapons for his new recruits."

There was a pause, then the former head of the Carolina Militia gave him an answer.

"I'd be interested if he'll pay cash."

"Give me your number. I'll call you back."

As he scribbled down the phone booth number, Comer grinned. He knew Byron Scott would pay him a ten percent commission for making the deal. The head of the Tax Resisters' Alliance needed weapons for his planned attacks on Internal Revenue Service offices in North Carolina, Tennessee, South Carolina and Alabama.

He dialed Scott's number at his farm near Birmingham.

CHAPTER FOURTEEN

General Mark Lawrence entered his large Pentagon office and walked to a window. Glancing outside, he could almost see the White House.

Suddenly looking older than his sixty-three years, the general locked the door behind him and stripped off his medal-heavy uniform jacket. Dropping it on one of the hooks of the coatrack near the door, he gazed around the room.

A lifetime of defending his country against all enemies was represented by the photographs, certificates and awards mounted on the walls. His history of service was profiled within the frames, from the day he graduated from West Point, to his service in Vietnam, right up to his current stateside post as head of military liaison between the White House and the Pentagon.

He had met them all—presidents, prime ministers, generals, admirals, even dictators, he remembered with a sour expression as he glanced at the photograph of the now dead Caribbean dictator who used a combination of voodoo and brutality to stay in power.

A lifetime of making certain that nothing, no one, could deliberately or foolishly betray the country, for selfish or supposedly noble reasons.

As he lowered himself into the chair behind his desk, Lawrence thought about the price he had paid for that decision—passed over for promotions and ridiculed by the press for speeches he had been making about elected officials who were giving the country away to the Communists, or letting too many nonwhites into a country for which he had fought so hard, for so long, to keep free.

Even his superiors had punished him for being so open about his views. They had pushed him aside so that he had no power within military community.

Or so the brownnosers thought.

What they didn't know was that he had a strong following among soldiers and patriots who believed that he was the only salvation for the country. They would find out soon enough that real Americans backed him, and not the current administration.

He glanced at a framed photograph on his desk of his dead wife and daughter, an attractive young woman in her early twenties. Leslie and Jody were the two people who would have understood how he felt. But they weren't here.

They hadn't been here for almost five years. The three of them had gone to dinner in San Francisco's Chinatown and got caught in the middle of a miniwar between the Crips, a black street gang, and the Red Dragon, a gang of Chinese teenage killers.

Leslie and Jody were killed as they reached down to sample the egg rolls in front of them, shredded by 9 mm high-velocity ammo shrieking into them from Uzi automatic pistols. Lawrence had been wounded, but managed to stay alive.

When his aide told him about the deaths of his wife and only child, he pledged to hunt down the killers and prevent any more like them from getting into the country.

One by one, men loyal to him tracked down members of the two gangs and killed them. The murderers were gone, but Lawrence realized more were being welcomed into the United States every day.

There was only one way to deal with them—keep them out of the country. His statements before congressional committees had no effect on the administration's immigration policies.

He decided that the only way to protect the country for whom he had given his life was to force the current President out of office, and to replace him with someone who could make the unpleasant but necessary decisions about forbidding nonwhites from migrating to the United States.

Perhaps someone like himself, who had seen firsthand how little life meant to these savages.

Until this Belasko had come into the picture, he had succeeded in showing up the current administration as the killers of those who disagreed with them, or as fools unable to cope with the rising violence in the country.

The polls proved he was gaining, even though his name was never mentioned. At the right moment, Senator Harvey McCutcheon would suggest that the country needed somebody strong like that great hero, Major General Mark Lawrence. He smiled at the vision and started to dwell on it, when he heard the knock at his door and sat up.

Bill Johnson entered the office. The well-dressed young man carried an expensive attaché case in his left hand. Behind him was Lawrence's second in command, Colonel Gregory Timmons.

Lawrence waited until the colonel closed the door behind him, then leaned back his head and closed his eyes. The only good thing about all of this was that the nightmare would be over in a few days.

Except in his memory.

Lawrence turned to Johnson. "What's the latest on the public-opinion front, Bill?"

Johnson, a specialist in conducting confidential political polls for many different candidates, opened his attaché case and pulled out a stack of papers.

"Do you want the details or just a general summation?"

"Give me the highlights for now. You can leave your report for me to read later."

Reading from the pages, Johnson summarized his findings.

"The public is becoming convinced that agents working for the federal government have become power mad. Waco, Ruby Ridge and a number of other incidents are turning the public away from backing the actions of the government."

"What about the Army?"

"They're way up in level of trust. Even with rumors that they are training some of these extremist groups in military tactics."

Lawrence pretended to be upset. As far as the pollster knew, the research he was reporting had been conducted for the White House.

He was certain the senator would be pleased. The campaign to discredit the men in power would make it possible for someone like the senator to run for the office of President.

And he, the senator had promised, would be invited to serve as the Chairman of the Joint Chiefs of Staff.

Lawrence knew the diggers of vulgar information in the media would bring up his history, especially the charges of brutality toward minority members of the Army. But so many years had passed since then that he didn't think any of the voters would care.

A question from the well-dressed pollster interrupted his thoughts. He again focused his attention on Johnson.

"Do you want an extra set of my report for the President?"

The general shook his head. "No. Officially, he doesn't know that such a poll has been conducted. And, of course, you will forget about it."

"Who gets my bill?"

"I do. It will be paid out of private funds."

It would be. Some of the large amounts of

money that been donated by most of the maligned citizen groups to the senator to continue his war with the administration would pay the invoice when it arrived.

Lawrence stood and held out his hand.

The young visitor understood. The meeting was over. That was one thing he liked about the former combat general. He didn't want to dwell over every little detail for hours, like other politicians.

"I'll leave my full report right here," Johnson said, placing the bound document on Lawrence's desk. "Call me if you need anything explained."

The general smiled and waited until his visitor left, closing the door behind him.

He turned to the colonel. "Anything to report?"

"The weapons delivered to the Carolina Militia by the White Aryan Resistance have been destroyed."

"Old news. I was told earlier by another contact. We've got some problems closer to home that need immediate handling."

Timmons sat up straight and nodded. "Name them, sir."

"The first one just left my office."

Timmons looked surprised. "Bill Johnson?"

"Would you consider him a security risk, Colonel?"

The junior officer weighed the question. "I think he's getting too close to figuring out that the government didn't order the polls. And he does talk to politicians—"

"Exactly," the general interrupted.

"When?"

"As soon as possible. Have your people make it look like an accident."

Timmons nodded. There wasn't much he could ask his former commanding officer about his orders. As usual, they were crisp and clear.

"Mr. Comer, the broadcaster, is aware of my identity," Timmons warned.

"For the moment, Marty Comer is a useful ally. When he no longer is..." The general didn't have to finish the thought.

"Anything else?"

"There is one last issue."

"Sir?"

"I understand that the men you hired failed to stop the mercenary, Mike Belasko, at the airport. Do you know who he is?"

"As you said, a mercenary recruited by this man, Brognola."

Lawrence shook his head. "His real name is Mack Bolan."

The colonel looked shocked. "But he's dead. He was killed in a gun battle several years ago. The sketch you furnished me of Belasko doesn't look a bit like Bolan."

"Cosmetic surgery, Timmons. A few men I know had run-ins with Bolan when he was Bolan—and since he became Belasko.

"I presume you've made it clear to all the men you've offered assistance to that if they reveal your name and identity—even if they are arrested and interrogated—they'll be dealt with harshly," Lawrence said in a grave tone of voice.

Both men remembered Lance Gault, the teenage leader of a skinhead gang for whom they obtained weapons two years earlier. He'd been arrested by the Los Angeles police when they found a quantity of stolen military rifles in the trunk of his car.

Under intense interrogation, Gault offered to provide the lawmen with the name of his supplier in exchange for a lighter sentence. The father of the skinhead leader posted bail, and while the officers met with a superior to get approval, someone killed the young man.

Timmons made sure that all of the groups who

dealt with him directly were sent copies of the news story about Gault's background, and death. He was positive that every one of them got the message.

"You're certain he's Mack Bolan?"

"Absolutely."

The colonel whistled softly. "Now I know why the men I hired failed."

"All it means is that you hired the wrong men, Colonel. This Bolan has been an irritation for a long time. Several valuable foreign contacts are no longer alive because of him. I don't care what it costs. I want him dead."

"He'll be eliminated, General. Just as soon as we find him," Timmons promised.

"Make it soon, Colonel. He's already cost us more than a hundred votes from members of the Carolina Militia. We will need every vote we can to put the *right* man into the White House in the next election."

Expressionless, the uniformed officer nodded again.

"It will be soon, sir. Even if I have to do it myself."

There was a knock at the door. Lawrence nodded to the colonel, who got up and opened it.

A tall, stout elderly man with bushy gray hair,

wearing a crumpled suit, walked past the Army officer and looked at Lawrence.

"We need to talk," he said.

"At your convenience, Senator."

"Now."

Lawrence turned to Timmons. "Keep me informed, Colonel."

The Army officer understood. The senator's meeting was a private one. He turned and left, closing the door behind him.

Harvey McCutcheon had been in Congress since 1968, over thirty years. Starting as a congressman, he served two terms, then ran for the Senate and won. As chairman of the Senate's subcommittee that concerned itself with abuse of power by the administration, as well as civil disobedience, he could conduct hearings on both topics at will.

"What the hell happened to get a lot of patriots slaughtered?"

Lawrence leaned back in his chair. "I assume you're speaking about the Smoky Mountains incident," he replied calmly.

"Yes," McCutcheon snapped. "I just heard from friends in North Carolina that the shipment of munitions destined for the Carolina Militia was destroyed."

The bushy-haired elected official used his eyes to examine every corner of the office.

"If you're looking for eavesdropping devices, there aren't any. One of my men—a specialist in such things—searches for such equipment every day."

The senator seemed mollified.

"What the hell happened?"

"The President formed an ad hoc committee to investigate organized warfare against the federal government."

"So what? He's formed a dozen such committees to look into things like tax evasion by members of Congress, influence of organized crime on elected officials. None of them amounted to a hill of beans."

"This time he's decided to do more than investigate. He's brought in a combat professional to take on the groups in battle."

"One man? Who is he? Superman?"

"Worse. He calls himself Mike Belasko, but he's really Mack Bolan."

"Never heard of him."

"That's because you stay behind the front lines. If you were up there where our people are doing everything they can to rid this country of the kind of administration we're stuck with, and get rid of the mongrels the government allows to seek refuge here, you'd know about Bolan."

He paused to let his statement sink in.

"His nickname is the Executioner. Does that give you some idea of what our people are facing?"

"Let's get rid of him before he does any more damage. I've got close to ten thousand people in my state alone who need weapons and ammunition to turn words into action. And every one of them represents a vote for our man."

"I wish it was that easy. We tried. At least one of my men hired professionals to kill him. This Bolan either leads a charmed life, or he's as good as his reputation."

"The party is beginning their search for a candidate who can win the presidential election. I think they would jump in a moment if the right man offered himself, no matter to what party he belongs. Our man has everything—experience, leadership, and he's someone the public trusts. Everything could go up in smoke if this Bolan character captures one of our people and makes him talk."

"There is no hard evidence. All we have to do is deny we even know of the accuser and his group."

The gray-haired senator smiled slyly.

"We need to make this Bolan sound like public enemy number one. Maybe Marty Comer could start the rumors flying that this Bolan is a mercenary hired by the administration to silence all opposition to their policies. And to add spice to the rumors, Comer and the other broadcasters could hint that he has gone out of control and become a ruthless killing machine."

Lawrence was grateful the senator was done with his angry monologue. Then he wondered if McCutcheon would ask him why Bolan was still alive.

He couldn't blame incompetence without sounding as if he was passing the buck. How could he explain that Bolan was more powerful than he had anticipated, based on his actions at the airport, the Commies' farm and the campsite?

The senator's face brightened as he leaned forward and stared at Lawrence.

"I think our first priority is to get rid of Bolan. You're the expert on killing." He looked apologetic. "I meant killing in combat, of course."

"We started out with three men trying to ambush Mack Bolan. We'll double the number next time. And if it's necessary, we'll send out a platoon."

McCutcheon pulled himself out of the easy chair that faced Lawrence's desk.

"I'll leave it up to you."

The retired general smiled. "Don't worry. Bolan is dead."

CHAPTER FIFTEEN

Hal Brognola watched as the tall gray-haired man got up from behind his desk and silently walked to the full-length windows. Alan Macomb sat silent in an easy chair and looked at the President. The Man stared into the darkness and shook his head, then turned to look at Brognola, who sat patiently in a leather chair and chewed on a long, unlit Honduran cigar.

"This has got to stop, Hal."

Hal Brognola wasn't sure what the Man meant, until the President added, "Show him, Alan."

The chief of staff handed Brognola a sheet of paper and took over the conversation. "Another shipment of military weapons has been stolen. This time, right from one of our arsenals." He glanced out of window. "And out there, groups are buying them to kill."

The President walked back to his desk and sat

down. "Five hijackings this month alone," he said. "What's the point of banning the sale of assault weapons? Anyone with the price can buy them on the street. It's a sad commentary on where the country is headed."

Now, Brognola understood why the President had gestured for him to follow him out of the high-level security-planning meeting when one of his aides entered the room and handed him the memorandum. The demand for powerful assault weapons had quadrupled in less than a year. And with the increased demand had come an increase in the number of attacks on military supply depots.

Macomb asked a question. "How do we stop them?"

The head of Stony Man Farm weighed the question for a long moment before answering. "Make it too expensive for them," he finally suggested.

"How?"

"Don't waste time arresting them so some fast-talking lawyer can get them out on bail."

"What's the alternative?"

Brognola remained silent.

"You've read the papers," the President reminded him. "The FBI, the U.S. Marshals and the

Bureau of Alcohol, Tobacco and Firearms are already under fire for brutality.'' He shook his head. ''We've always had rogue policemen, rogue state troopers, rogue FBI and Secret Service agents. Even rogue congressmen. I don't know how much of it is true, but we can't risk committing them to another charge of deliberate murder.''

''I have a possible solution.''

The gray-haired man loosened his tie and stared at the Stony Man Farm chief.

''Who?''

''Striker.''

The President nodded. ''I like that.''

''Striker?'' Macomb queried.

''It's need-to-know, Alan,'' the President stated.

He stood and paced the length of the room before he spoke again. ''The FBI's already involved in catching the hijackers on this one, so you're going to have to work them and other agencies this time, Hal.''

The expression on Brognola's face made it plain he wasn't thrilled with the prospect. ''What other agencies?''

''The Treasury's Alcohol, Tobacco and Firearms unit, possibly the DEA. There might be others.'' The tall gray-haired man understood how the head of the Sensitive Operations Group felt about exposing his men to interagency rivalries. "I want you to coordinate the project. Any idea who you'll assign?"

Brognola stood. "Not assign—ask, Mr. President," he corrected. "I'm hoping Striker will take this on in addition to what he's doing for us."

"You know that if he's caught, we'll deny any affiliation with the government?"

"As always, Mr. President."

The President stood and held out his hand. Brognola walked to the desk and shook it.

"What a thankless job you have, Hal."

"There are compensations."

The tall man looked at him curiously. "I can't think of one."

"Serving this nation by getting rid of vermin."

The door to the Oval Office opened, and the President's personal secretary entered.

"Excuse me, Mr. President, but there's a call for Mr. Brognola."

"Take a number and I'll call whoever it is back," the head of Stony Man Farm growled.

"The man told me to tell you it was Striker calling," she added.

Brognola stood.

"Where can I take the call, Mr. President?"

"Take the call here if you don't mind."

The big Fed waited for the woman to leave, then reached for the phone on the massive desk.

"Brognola here."

SITTING BEHIND THE DESK in the sheriff's private office, Bolan checked to make certain he was alone. Handler had left the small room and gone out to talk to his men.

The soldier gave his report. "You've got a leak back there."

"How do you know?"

"There was a reception committee waiting for me at the Asheville airport, and a large squad of the Carolina Militia was hidden in bushes on the farm anticipating my arrival."

"I heard how you handled both situations. Any idea who was behind it?"

"Some suspicions, but nothing definite. The members of the airport reception committee were professionals."

"Mafia?"

"More like mercenaries."

"Another load of military hardware was hijacked, and the FBI and other federal agencies are getting ready to battle the hijackers. They're setting up a roadblock."

Handler walked into his office and overheard the conversation.

"Want company?" the sheriff inquired.

"Hold on," Bolan said into the phone, and turned to the sheriff.

"I need you right here. The Carolina Militia isn't the only hate group in your county. And the Montagnards are going to need you to help them get started again."

Handler sighed. "I hate to admit it, but you're right. But if you ever need an extra pair of hands, you know my telephone number."

Bolan waited until the sheriff left the office.

He spoke into the phone. "Where are they setting up?"

"About forty miles from Haywood." Brognola gave Bolan the location. "A local sheriff called the Raleigh office of the FBI about a gang of bikers escorting a large truck through his town. He happened to check the truck's license plates. It was reported stolen and the driver found murdered.

"Where were you heading?" the big Fed asked.

"I was going to catch up with a radio commentator named Marty Comer. He seems to have some nasty friends."

"He's also a rattlesnake with powerful connections. If you have to ace him, there'll be a lot of breast beating in Congress." There was silence for a moment. Then Brognola added, "The bikers who hijacked the shipment all belong to that white-supremacist group of bikers mentioned at our meet with the President, the White Aryan Resistance. The FBI has an undercover agent with them, so we know their route and where to stop them."

"I've had a run-in with them. Bunch of racist killers." Bolan smiled without mirth.

"I guess Comer will have to wait. Can you alert the various law-enforcement people a Justice agent is on the way? Some of the bikers might have some information I can use."

"What kind of information do you want?"

"Who's the chief honcho in this civil war."

Brognola came right to the point. "Got any suspicions?"

"It's not you or the President, so that leaves Alan Macomb, the chief of staff, who knew where I was heading, and when."

"Not that it means anything by itself," Brognola said, "but I've known Alan Macomb for a lot of years. As far as I can tell, he's always been a straight shooter."

"Knowing you, you're not going to give up

trying to find out the source of the leak,'' Bolan replied.

''Right. And I'll ask the Man to contact the FBI about you. It will carry more weight. And stay hard, Striker.''

Bolan knew Brognola's last words were a testament of their long friendship.

Stay hard. Stay alive.

The Executioner hung up the phone.

It was time to introduce the WAR bikers to the kind of hell they'd never seen before.

CHAPTER SIXTEEN

Lightly gripping the wheel of the panel moving truck, Sterno kept humming. The bearded biker glanced in the large side-view mirror. A long line of White Aryan Resistance members was riding on each side of the vehicle.

He glanced at Lodge, sitting next to him. He hoped the head biker would decide to get back on asphalt. He was getting tired of bouncing around the rubble-filled dirt roads. He was positive the rest of the gang felt the same way.

They'd been skirting large towns and cities by traveling on ungraded roads that existed on only the most detailed maps. They were heading for a supposedly deserted warehouse where their new customer was waiting.

Forty miles outside of Haywood, Lodge called for a short break in a rest area. He sauntered to a pay phone, and he placed a call to Marty Comer.

"This guy we're going to meet. He knows the price?"

"To the penny. He's expecting you later tonight. Did you lose any men?"

"Nobody. I was just checking in."

"I'm glad you did," Comer commented. "My Washington contact just called."

"That soldier boy—Timmons?"

"Yes. He wanted to warn both of us about some big bad hero named Mack Bolan, who he thinks had something to do with the Carolina Militia killings. Timmons thinks he might be tracking you."

"Doesn't matter. Haven't met the man yet who can stand up to my boys."

"Don't get cocky," Comer warned. "This Bolan is supposed to be something else."

"What he'll be," Lodge snarled, "is dead. And that's a promise you can take to the bank."

THE GROUP OF BIKERS had parked their Harley-Davidson motorcycles around the truck. Large men with beards, and swathed in black leather jackets, dismounted. The leather-jacketed women who had been riding behind them got off and rapidly disappeared into the woods surrounding them.

"Tell your old ladies they got ten minutes to piss," Lodge warned his men when he returned from the pay phone.

Poker, the enforcer of the gang, sidled over to Lodge. "Enough time for a drink?"

"Save it till after we dump this load. Then we'll have us a real party."

Connection joined them. "How much longer before we get there, big man?"

This was Connection's first robbery. Lodge could see the excitement in the kid's eyes. "Soon enough. Just you make sure you got enough stuff to keep us happy for a couple of days."

Connection grinned. "All I gotta do is make a couple of calls."

"It'll have to wait until we get to a pay phone."

Connection nodded happily. "I can't wait to make that call."

Lodge looked back at Larry Potter, sitting between the two scantily clad teenaged bimbos who'd been traveling with the gang in the rear of the truck. Behind the trio were Sterno's and his bikes, safely chained to anchors against the rear walls.

The Carolina Militia chief grinned at him.

Lodge asked, "Feel like stretching your legs?"

"I think the three of us will just stay back here." He glanced at the two abundantly bosomed girls. "Right?"

He had given each of the pair several hundred dollars so they could go shopping for new clothes when they got to a decent-sized town.

The redhead and blonde nodded and smiled at each other.

Fifteen minutes later, the bikers were on the move again. The county road was deserted. As the White Aryan Resistance moved across it, they could see the handful of impoverished farms that bordered the two lanes. Even in the dark they could see the huge outcroppings that made farming an almost impossible task.

Lodge had spent his childhood on just such a farm, living with a drunken uncle who thought the way to raise his nephew was to beat him into adulthood with a thick strap.

Each biker had a loaded automatic assault rifle, conveniently anchored close enough to be reached in case of an emergency. Nobody expected they would be needed, but Lodge insisted they carry them, especially when they were going out on a raid, or coming back from one.

Inside the truck cab, Sterno started to hum again.

"Keep your eyes on the road," Lodge warned, then turned and looked at Larry Potter. The head of the Carolina Militia still looked happy as the two teenagers let him run his hands over their breasts.

Lodge turned back and picked up the CB microphone and pushed in the button. He knew each of his bikers had a CB transceiver constantly tuned to the same channel.

"Anyone who falls behind is on his own, so keep your minds on the road and save thinking about partying for later," he warned.

GLANCING OUT HIS WINDOW, the biker leader saw the young blond girl who rode behind Connection kissing his neck.

"Connection, tell that bitch to save turning you on for when we get there," Lodge shouted angrily into the microphone.

Connection slowed his bike until he was alongside the passenger's door of the truck and waved his acknowledgment.

"That goes for the bitches on the rest of the bikes," he shouted over the radio. He turned his head and glared at the redhead and blonde who were sitting on the floor with their backs against the two Harley-Davidson Sportsters parked behind the front seats. He caught the redhead starting to take her clothes off.

"Hey, bitch," he snapped, "you leave Potter alone till we get done with our business. Then I'll show you how we party."

Sterno grinned at Lodge's promise. The girls behind them were young, and new to the gang. But Sterno had been with Lodge for the past five years. He could remember some parties that had gotten too wild even for him. And none of the girls with them back then was as young and as full of energy as these two.

He glanced around the well-appointed interior. "Guy who we stole this truck from sure liked his luxury," Sterno observed.

They had found the truck driver on the side of a small highway where he had parked to catch a short nap. Dirt Bag had cut his throat before the man could open his eyes, then lifted a nearby sewer cover and shoved the body down the wide pipe to give the rats below a feast of fresh meat.

He glanced at Lodge. "You gonna call the talk man and let him know we're on our way?"

The head biker glanced back at where the surplus dealer was sitting. "Potter called him before we left that hick North Carolina burg. Comer gave him directions to the customer. We'll be there before too long.''

The only thing Lodge wasn't sure about was if Byron Scott was a government plant. The Feds had tried to get someone inside before, but sooner or later the snitch gave himself away.

If Scott was a government plant, Lodge had enough trained guns to deal with the problem.

''How much you think we'll get for this load?''

''We'll haggle with the customer.''

Sterno nodded toward where Potter was busily engaged with the two girls.

''What's the split between him and us?''

Lodge grinned. ''There isn't gonna be a split.''

Sterno looked concerned. ''Is the talk man gonna be ticked?''

The head biker winked. ''Accidents happen.''

Sterno was about to needle the head of the White Aryan Resistance, then caught himself. As well as he knew Lodge, he was never certain when Lodge was kidding and when he was serious.

The one thing he knew was that Lodge didn't like to be teased. Sterno had been with the White Aryan Resistance for a year when he first realized how the other man hated needling. In response to a drunken dig by the man who'd been the gang's president at the time, Lodge smiled and pulled out the large double-edged knife he carried in his right boot, then rammed it into the other man's stomach.

He changed the subject. "Hey, what do you think that is up ahead?"

A peculiar flickering glow rose just over the hill they approached. Lodge turned and stared through the windshield as they began the climb.

"I don't know. Kind of strange. Been on this road a dozen times and never seen it before." He kept staring at the glow as they reached the peak of the hill. Suddenly, he muttered a curse, threw his hand on the horn button on the steering wheel and blasted out the arranged warning to the rest of the gang to grab their weapons and scatter.

"Goddamn it, it's a fuckin' roadblock! How'd they know where to find us?"

Lodge stared at the driver. No, he didn't think it was Sterno. They'd been together too long. It had to be one of the newer members who ratted.

Someone like Connection.

Lodge shook his head. Now he would have to find a new source for drugs.

THE EXECUTIONER HAD shown up a half hour earlier and introduced himself to Rick Braddock, head of the special FBI team at the roadblock.

"Got the word from headquarters you were going to join us, Belasko. Just take cover. We've got all the help we need."

Bolan glanced at the dozen state police troopers, armed with combat shotguns and assault rifles, and teams from the Alcohol, Tobacco and Firearms unit of the Treasury Department, and the six FBI snipers waiting behind a barricade formed of police vehicles.

Two men moved quietly behind the soldier.

Bolan could sense somebody behind him. Whirling on his left foot, he drew the silenced Beretta and started to bring it into target acquisition. Then he spotted the deputy sheriff uniforms both men were wearing, and eased his finger from the trigger.

"Make some kind of a noise next time you show up," Bolan commented. "I almost shot both of you."

The two lawmen smiled at each other, then introduced themselves. The thinner of the pair spoke. "I'm Billy Proudfoot." He pointed to the heavyset deputy who wore his hair long and tied back with a rubber band. "This is Frank Tallchief. We're cousins."

He looked at their features. "Cherokees?"

"Yeah," Tallchief answered. "We live up there on the reservation." He pointed to the steep hills that surrounded the area.

Bolan looked at the two men. They seemed relaxed, as if the battle were just a lark.

"The guys on those bikes are killers," Bolan warned.

"So we figured," Proudfoot commented.

The news didn't seem to faze them. The Executioner changed the subject. "Just get here?"

"We've been here for almost an hour scouting the area. All we know is that the sheriff told us to represent the county here. We've been trying to figure out what this is all about," Proudfoot said.

"Did you figure it out?"

"Nope," the other deputy answered. "Not unless you're after those psycho bikers, escorting a large truck, and coming in this direction."

"That's what it's all about," Bolan said.

"That's what we thought," Proudfoot replied, adding, "There are a lot of them, and from what we could see, they're all armed."

"They're also a gang of white supremacists," Bolan explained.

"This is Mike Belasko," the FBI task force

interrupted, introducing Bolan. "He's been sent from Washington, D.C., to make sure we do a good job." Then he walked away.

"From the way you handled that Beretta, I don't think that's the only reason you're here," Frank Tallchief commented.

Bolan could see the glow of headlights in the distance. It was time to get ready.

"Excuse me. I'll be right back."

"We've got something to do to stir up a little excitement while you're gone," Tallchief said, leading his partner up a steep hill.

Bolan went back to the rental car and slipped out of his outer clothes. The blacksuit was more appropriate for hard night combat. He opened his canvas carryall and grabbed an M-16 A-2 fitted with an M-203 grenade launcher, taken from the battle at the Montagnard farm, as well as his pair of handguns and the Applegate-Fairbairn combat blade.

The Uzi was less useful in the kind of battle the soldier anticipated, but he slung the Israeli-made submachine gun over a shoulder, then loaded extra magazines for his weapons in his combat vest pockets. Six 40 mm delayed-fuse fragmentation grenades were clipped to the outside of the sleeveless battle garment.

He started to leave, then changed his mind and reached back into the canvas bag to extract a small brick of C-4 plastique and a miniaturized detonator and timer.

Then he made his way back to where the two deputies had been standing. They had disappeared. Moments later, the two men joined him.

"I haven't seen anyone carrying that much armament since Desert Storm," Tallchief stated.

"Looks like you're ready to bag some game," Proudfoot said, impressed.

The Executioner changed the subject. "You were saying something about stirring up some excitement. How?"

"Show him," Proudfoot told his cousin.

Tallchief held up a thick canvas sack. Something inside was making a strange noise.

Bolan started to reach for the bag. "What've you got inside?"

The deputy stopped him. "I don't think you want to put your hand in there."

Tallchief held the bag open while Proudfoot shone a light at the inside. Glaring up at them was a pair of mountain rattlesnakes shaking their tails in warning.

Proudfoot explained, "We know a lot about racists. When we were kids, we got tired of being pushed around by the white bullies who went to the same consolidated high school. So we started picking up bags full of these things and dropping them in the back seats of our tormentors' cars.''

"Sure got them to stop picking on us," Proudfoot added.

Bolan looked at them. "What do you plan on doing with them?"

"We'll collect a few more, then slip behind the bikers and drop them in a couple of saddlebags. If we get enough of them, we drop a few inside the truck." Tallchief grinned. "Never met anybody yet who felt real good about having one of these as a traveling companion."

The soldier couldn't suppress a grin as he studied the canvas sack. "Just one thing—don't get caught doing it."

"We haven't been yet," Proudfoot said, signaling to his cousin it was time to get busy again.

"Meet you out there," Bolan said, pointing in the direction of the phalanx of lights coming at them.

The two deputies vanished into the darkness.

Bolan wasn't sure he approved of what the pair was planning to do, but he was glad they were on his side.

PLAY "LUCKY 7" AND GET
THREE FREE GIFTS!

HOW TO PLAY:

1. With a coin, carefully scratch off the silver box at the right. Then check the claim c to see what we have for you — **FREE BOOKS** and a gift — **ALL YOURS! ALL FREE**

2. Send back this card and you'll get hot-off-the-press Gold Eagle® books, never be published! These books have a cover price of $4.50 or more each in the U.S. and $5.2 more each in Canada, but they are yours to keep absolutely free.

3. There's no catch. You're u no obligation to buy anything. charge nothing — ZERO — your first shipment. And you c have to make any minimum nur of purchases — not even one!

4. The fact is thousands of readers enjoy receiving books by mail from the Gold E Reader Service™. They like the convenience of home delivery…they like getting the new novels BEFORE they're available in stores…and they love our discount prices!

5. We hope that after receiving your free books you'll want to remain a subscriber. the choice is yours — to continue or cancel, any time at all! So why not take us up on invitation, with no risk of any kind. You'll be glad you did!

YOURS FREE!

PLAY LUCKY 7 FOR THIS EXCITING FREE GIFT!

THIS SURPRISE MYSTERY GIFT COULD BE YOURS FREE WHEN YOU PLAY

LUCKY 7!

NO COST! NO OBLIGATION TO BUY!
NO PURCHASE NECESSARY!

The Gold Eagle Reader Service™ — Here's how it works:

Accepting your 2 free books and gift places you under no obligation to buy anything. You may keep the books and gift and return the shipping statement marked "cancel." If you do not cancel, about a month later we'll send you 6 additional novels and bill you just $26.70* — that's a savings of 15% off the cover price of all 6 books! And there's no extra charge for shipping! You may cancel at any time, but if you choose to continue, every other month we'll send you 6 more books, which you may either purchase at the discount price or return to us and cancel your subscription.

*Terms and prices subject to change without notice. Sales tax applicable in N.Y. Canadian residents will be charged applicable provincial taxes and GST.

If offer card is missing write to: Gold Eagle Reader Service, 3010 Walden Ave., P.O. Box 1867, Buffalo, NY 14240-1867

BUSINESS REPLY MAIL
FIRST-CLASS MAIL   PERMIT NO. 717   BUFFALO, NY

POSTAGE WILL BE PAID BY ADDRESSEE

GOLD EAGLE READER SERVICE
3010 WALDEN AVE
PO BOX 1867
BUFFALO NY 14240-9952

NO POSTAGE
NECESSARY
IF MAILED
IN THE
UNITED STATES

SOMETHING WAS WRONG with the floor of the truck. It was supposed to be made of wood and metal, but it felt soft and seemed to move. Larry Potter started to reach down to feel it, when he heard dry rattling noises near his right foot.

He jumped onto his seat. Something was on the floor. Something that twisted and moved. He looked down and gasped.

Coiled and staring up at him was the largest, meanest snake he had ever seen. It kept forcing its forked tongue out of its ugly mouth and spitting.

For a moment, he was paralyzed. Slowly, the numbness of fear ebbed and he realized suddenly he was only a few feet from painful death.

Ignoring the two teenage girls, Potter tore at the rear doors. The rattler, in its desperate effort to get away from the large, strange figure that blocked its escape, sank its fangs into him.

Flinging the truck doors open, the surplus dealer jumped out and hit the hard dirt road with the back of his neck. There was a clearly audible snap.

His eyes glazed in terror for eternity, Larry Potter lay dead in the dirt road, unnoticed and unmourned.

BRADDOCK COULDN'T TAKE his eyes off the man the White House had sent. Not only was he tall and powerfully built, but also there was something about Mike Belasko that alerted the FBI man that the President's representative was more than just an observer.

He looked as if he had been in a lot of battles and come out of all of them the victor. He was dressed in a one-piece black uniform, which resembled a close-fitting raid suit, and he looked like someone who could help them stop the horde of killers that was the WAR gang.

"I thought you were just going to be an observer," the head of the FBI team commented. "You any good with those weapons?"

"We'll find out soon enough," Bolan replied.

"Hopefully, not we—them," the FBI man said. Then he walked away to respond to a gesture from one of the lawmen hiding behind the parked cars.

The Executioner melted into the thick brush that flanked the roadway.

CHAPTER SEVENTEEN

The bikers stopped their motorcycles on the dirt road, yelling at the girls they'd been carrying to run for cover, and yanked out their weapons.

Ahead of them, a solid wall of police vehicles, with lights flashing, blocked the road. "Stop for a second," Lodge shouted to Sterno.

Then he jumped out of the truck cab. The bike gang looked at their leader.

"Hit 'em hard with everything you got, and make sure none of them leave here alive," he shouted.

A DARK SHADOW APPEARED behind the truck carrying the weapons and glanced inside. The cargo was perfect for what the Executioner planned to do.

Shouldering the M-16, Bolan slid under the vehicle and planted the C-4 plastique on the undercarriage, then set the timer and attached both it and the detonator to the gray block of plastic explosive.

He pulled himself out from under the truck and fisted the silenced Uzi submachine gun.

Now it was time to get the show on the road.

LODGE CLIMBED BACK in the cab and looked at the bearded driver.

"Get this damned rig moving!"

Sterno reacted instantly. The rig bounced as he rumbled on the uneven dirt of the shoulder.

"Keep driving," Lodge yelled, climbing over the seat to the back of the truck.

The two teenage girls cowered in terror. They'd come along for the drugs and party Lodge had promised them. Neither had been warned that they might be facing flying bullets from police guns.

Screams of panic erupted from the leather-clad women who rode behind the last five bikers as rattlesnakes crawled out of the opened saddle bags and onto their legs.

One of them, a heavyset blonde, dived from the rear of a bike. A second—her eyes widening in fear—grabbed the snake and tried to throw it to the ground. Desperate to escape, the rattler twisted its body and rammed its fangs into the woman's neck.

Two of the biker companions escaped death when the serpents in their saddlebags managed to wriggle out and fall onto the dirt road.

The fifth grabbed the rattler and tried to throw it from the bike. The poisonous snake landed instead on Poker's leather-clad vest.

"A rattlesnake!" his woman yelled.

Poker reached behind to pull the slithering creature from him and was rewarded with the rattler's large volume of venom. Screaming for help, the bearded biker opened up his engine and crashed into the two bikes in front of him. All three spun out of control and burst into flames, consuming the bikers and their women in the fiery inferno that erupted when sparking metal contacted leaking gasoline.

BOLAN KNEW the deputies had worked their magic. He made a rapid decision. Gripping the silenced Beretta in his free hand, he decided to get the battle started.

He hosed the area in front of him. As 9 mm lead flew from the Uzi SMG and shattered two bikers, their motorcycles smashed into the side of the fast-moving truck and their decimated bodies tumbled into the road.

One of the still living bikers turned his head and saw the dark figure of what looked like the reincarnation of the Devil. He shouted a warning to the gang member next to him, who managed to train his Tec-9 on Bolan and loose a burst.

A pair of metal-jacketed rounds tore into Bolan's shoulder and out the rear. Falling to the ground, the Executioner forced himself to pull out of the roadway and roll into the bushes.

He knew he would soon pass out from the loss of blood.

A pair of shadows emerged from the brush. The soldier tried to reach for the Desert Eagle in his waist holster, then recognized the two deputies.

"Sorry we missed the fun, but we just got here," Proudfoot whispered.

Tallchief spotted the blood leaking from Bolan's shoulder wounds. "Man, you need doctoring," he commented.

He nodded to his partner.

One of them grabbed the emptied SMG, then both of them pulled Bolan to his feet and walked him in the direction of the police vehicles.

CONCENTRATING THEIR thoughts on the battle that was starting, the rest of the bikers hadln't noted the demise of the rear bikers.

The teenage girls started to scream when they heard the whining slugs of high-powered lead bang against the truck body. From somewhere outside, they heard the sound of rapid-firej automatic guns rupture the air.

l "Jam on the brakes!" Lodge shouted.

Sterno rammed his foot down, sgghlamming the two bikes in back and the screaming girls against the far truck wall.

"Get a gun!" Lodge ordered, grabbing a short ugly Uzi automatic assault rifle from the floor of the cab.

Sterno reached down and picked up one of the Tec-9 assault pistols they'd hijacked the month before. He kicked off the safety and threw open the driver's door.

Rolling to the ground, he turned and let loose a burst of searing lead at two men, leading the assault on foot. Both wore jackets that identified them as FBI agents. Flanking them was a pair of men wearing ATF jackets, and a dozen state and county officers.

Like a football team on the offensive, they rushed the gang. Instead of a football, each of them carried an automatic weapon that belched smoking pellets of death.

The White Aryan Resistance responded with a rain of gunfire. They stood their ground, spraying the oncoming men with waves of 9 mm and .45-caliber slugs. Each of them fought back desperately, knowing that to be caught could mean a death penalty for previous killings or, even worse, punishment at the hands of Lodge.

Like the others, Sterno locked his finger on the trigger of his Tec-9, panning it slowly from left to right at the uniformed officers who were moving toward him. For a moment, it looked as if the earth had opened up and spewed cops from every direction.

Behind him, he could sense Lodge jumping from the opened rear of the truck. "Drop down!" Lodge yelled.

Sterno knew better than to ask why. He threw himself to the ground.

The gang leader carried a full array of arms. Holding a 40 mm MM-1 multigrenade launcher against his shoulder, he aimed quickly and fired an incendiary grenade at a rapidly approaching trio of uniformed men. The grenade exploded with a loud whoosh as it slammed into the uniformed officer who led the attack. A shower of flames turned his body into a charring torch as he fell to the ground, screaming in pain. The other three agents made the mistake of stopping to try to help him.

Lodge aimed his weapon and launched a second incendiary grenade.

In the distance, he could hear the sounds of gunfire being exchanged. There was no way of knowing who was winning.

"Get me that tube from the back," he ordered.

Sterno dropped his gun and rushed into the truck. He came out with a Honeywell rocket launcher, fitted with a HEAT missile.

Sterno handed him the grenade launcher, and Lodge peered inside. The sleek rocket was already in place. He balanced the weapon on his shoulder.

A hundred yards in front of them were the police and federal law-enforcement vehicles that had blocked their journey. He could see that some of the lawmen were getting into cars, ready to launch a massive attack on his men and him.

If he could stop their assault, he and the others who still lived would have time to get away before reinforcements could be summoned. He hated wasting something as hard to come by as a high-powered missile on cops.

The burly gang leader peered through the sighting device mounted on top of the tube, ignoring the line of heavily armed police vehicles heading toward him.

The two teenage girls had climbed from the back of the truck and now cowered in the cab behind Sterno, holding on to each other for safety.

Unaware of their presence, the bearded biker watched as Lodge started to count under his breath. "Five, four, three, two, one." Then he tugged on the triggerlike device that launched the rocket.

Both he and Sterno watched as the small missile raced toward the parked vehicles. Behind them, they could hear the screams of the girls as the exploding propellant sprayed its fiery residue over them.

Sterno turned quickly and watched as the screaming girls burned to death. Lodge ignored their cries and watched with fascination as the missile made contact with the vehicles.

The missile cored through the steel of two of the cars it hit. Suddenly, the flaming vehicles exploded, spraying glowing bits of metal and glass in every direction for thirty yards. The shouts and screams of the men and women caught in the conflagration died away as quickly as they had started.

Lodge barely glanced at the burned bodies of the girls behind him as he handed the launcher to Sterno.

"Load that thing in back and let's get our asses out of here before the cops get their shit together," he said as he climbed into the truck.

Sterno rushed to obey him. He slammed the rear doors shut, sidestepping the remains of the two girls, then jumped into the cab of the truck and turned on the engine. Lodge leaned over and hit the horn with the signal that meant they were getting out of there.

Leading the way, the truck raced forward, twisting and pitching as Sterno struggled with the steering wheel. Behind them, the still functioning bikes twisted and turned over the uneven terrain, desperately trying to keep up with the truck.

Lodge looked into his side-view mirror. A dozen cops chased after them on foot. Their vehicles had been destroyed in the rocket explosion.

A pair of FBI snipers, with long-range assault rifles, knelt and picked off several bikers and the women who rode behind them. The bikes spun out of control, one of them charging into the side of a racing bike and propelling the biker and his woman in the air, then back down to the ground—dead.

"Head for the road," Lodge snapped to Sterno, then repeated his order to his gang members.

The few survivors responded to his CB radio call. Most of them had been injured or wounded, most not so seriously they couldn't travel.

The remaining members of the gang didn't answer Lodge's call. He called out their names again and asked if anyone knew what had happened to them or their women.

Each had been killed in the battle, someone told him.

"Dirt Bag here," a voice reported. "I got one of the guys slung across the back of my bike."

"Think he's gonna make it?"

"Not a chance in hell."

"Dump him," the furious head of the bike gang spit into the microphone. "I suppose the cops got Connection."

"No, I trashed him," Dirt Bag reported. "I caught him using a flashlight to signal the cops. Son of a bitch was a snitch."

"I thought so!" Lodge muttered. "Now we gotta find somebody else to get us dope." He made a face, then added, "Let's get out of here. We'll figure out a destination when we get out of this area. Plans have changed."

Sterno agreed. "I just wanna get back up north and get shit-faced for a week."

"After we get rid of our cargo."

"Hey, boss, that can wait," Sterno protested.

The bearded biker could see the anger rising in the leader of the White Aryan Resistance.

"I was only suggesting that we could all use a little break," Sterno said, with the hint of a whine in his voice.

Lodge was in no mood to argue. He raised the 9 mm Tec-9 he held in his right hand and emptied the clip into the biker's face. Blood and bits of tissue and bone splattered all over him. Ignoring the gore, he stared at the shattered body that fell to the ground.

"Tell it to those two teenyboppers," Lodge snarled.

THE TWO DEPUTIES PLACED him on the front passenger's seat of his Jeep. Proudfoot examined the rapidly bleeding wounds.

"Frank can help out temporarily."

"Thanks for the offer, but I think this is going to need a real doctor's attention—when I get the time."

Bolan noticed that Tallchief had vanished. He returned carrying a large bag. Opening it, he took out a syringe and a vial. Filling the hypodermic, he started to insert the sharp point into the soldier's arm.

"Hold on," the Executioner snapped. "You know what you're doing?"

"Sure."

"It's okay, Mr. Belasko. Frank was a senior medic during the Saddam embarrassment," Proudfoot explained.

Bolan relaxed and let the former medic cleanse and suture the wounds.

"Damn," Proudfoot muttered to himself. "Bastards got away with the truck."

"They won't get far," Bolan announced.

The deputy stared at him. "How come?"

A tremendous explosion thundered somewhere along the road ahead, followed by a series of smaller explosions that lit up the sky.

"We'd appreciate it if you didn't mention to the sheriff what you did," Proudfoot stated. "He gets kind of upset when something happens to county property, like the road."

"Meantime, we better haul you back to the reservation."

"Not now."

"What I did was temporary," Tallchief

warned. "There's an old man up there who can get you back in action in a hurry."

As the soldier began to fade into unconsciousness from the loss of blood, he glanced at the blurry images of the two deputies. They were resourceful, capable and trustworthy. He thought of recommending them to Brognola.

"There's a man who could use guys like you on his team," Bolan said, slurring his words.

"I like big-league rat hunting." Proudfoot grinned. He looked at his partner. "You think we should consider the offer?"

"Sure," Tallchief replied. "If you're willing to tell my wife about it."

"Those two women give a new definition to the word *mean*," Proudfoot said, shaking his head. "I'd rather stay alive."

Bolan didn't hear Tallchief's answer. He had slipped into oblivion.

CHAPTER EIGHTEEN

Bolan woke up with a start. He saw the elderly Native American standing over him, holding some kind of tool in his hand, and thought he was still dreaming. The searing pain in his left shoulder told him he wasn't.

"Who are you?"

The elderly Cherokee placed a hand on Bolan's forehead and grunted.

Behind him, Bolan saw a pair of familiar faces—Billy Proudfoot and Frank Tallchief.

Bolan realized the elderly Cherokee wore a long white coat. A young woman entered the room, and she, too, wore white.

He turned his head and gestured to the deputies. "Where am I?"

"Cherokee Clinic. We hauled you back to the reservation so the docs could fix you up."

The soldier glanced at the pair of white-coats. "Doctors?" he asked.

"Dr. Longfellow and my wife, Dr. Proudfoot," the deputy explained with a smile. Then he added, "He uses a combination of modern medicine and ancient Cherokee cures in his treatment of patients."

Bolan realized he had to be on the large Cherokee reservation he had passed on his way to the Montagnards' farm.

"The bag in my Jeep. I had some things in it...." he started to say.

"Looked like enough to wipe out a lot of bad guys," Proudfoot commented. "We got it safely stored for you. And we had one of the ladies on the reservation patch up your long black underwear."

Bolan would have smiled, but he was too weary. "How long have I been here?"

Frank Tallchief thought about the question.

"Probably a day and a half."

The soldier thought about Hal Brognola. He had promised to check in daily with the head of Stony Man Farm.

"I've got to make a call."

"No calls," Billy Proudfoot's wife announced.

"This is urgent. A lot of people will die if I don't call in."

The doctor looked at her husband, who nodded.

"Belasko is supposed to be some kind of big deal in Washington, D.C., Sally. Better let him make the call."

"You make it short, and you stay in bed until I tell you that it's all right to get up. Understood?"

When Bolan nodded, the doctor handed him the phone on the nightstand.

DESPITE THE LATE HOUR, Hal Brognola was still at his Justice Department office.

Bolan dialed directly to the big Fed's private line, and Brognola picked it up on the first ring.

As he always did when he was weighing a serious problem, Brognola chewed on an unlit cigar and considered the Executioner's report.

"First there was the attack at the airport. It was made to look like a kidnapping, but one of the killers had a sketch of me in his pocket.

"Then there's the militiamen hiding at the Montagnard farm. I don't think they were waiting for the sheriff to show up. They could have killed him at any time," the soldier added.

"So we have a leak. We know that. We just

can't figure out who it is. I don't buy Alan Macomb. No way."

"You're going to have to figure it out, Hal," the Executioner replied. "I've got an appointment with a man who isn't expecting me."

"Who?"

"Do you really want to know?"

Brognola was silent, then answered. "No, I suppose not."

"The fewer people who know where I'm going, the more chance that I'll get there alive," Bolan agreed.

"Stay hard, Striker," the Stony Man Farm head said. "We've got a long way to go before we're rid of the termites."

After he hung up, Bolan thought about Brognola's last words. He had found a perfect way to describe the hate groups. Termites, gnawing at the foundation of the country.

There was only one way to deal with termites— especially human ones.

Exterminate them.

BILLY PROUDFOOT ENTERED the small hospital room. "Done with your call?"

Bolan nodded, then asked, "Can you bring me my bag?"

"If you need shaving gear, I can lend you some of mine."

The soldier shook his head. "Just the bag."

The deputy was about to turn down the request until he looked into Bolan's hard eyes. The expression on his face was one of grim determination.

This was not someone Billy Proudfoot wanted to argue with—about anything.

Minutes later, Bolan checked the contents of his bag. Someone had cleaned his weapons. The two deputies, he decided.

The neatly mended blacksuit was folded and shoved into a corner. His outer garments were washed, ironed and carefully folded.

With a great deal of pain and effort, Bolan pulled himself into a sitting position.

The two deputies entered the room.

"Where do you think you're going?" Frank Tallchief asked.

"First, the bathroom to get cleaned up."

"Then?"

"I've got to see a man about a broadcast," Bolan replied as he dragged himself out of the hospital bed.

The two deputies looked at each other. Proudfoot turned to the Executioner.

"It wouldn't happen to be Marty Comer, the psycho talk-show character?"

Bolan didn't reply. This was his war.

Tallchief shook his head. "Comer is a folk hero to a lot of crazies who like his message of racism and hate. And you think you're going to stop him?"

"Yeah, I do."

"One man against thousands of nuts." A skeptical look crossed Proudfoot's face. "You don't have a snowball's chance in hell of succeeding."

"I can try," Bolan replied.

"You're on a suicide mission. The odds are against you. Why don't you pack your bag and go back to D.C.?"

"Like you said. Not a snowball's chance in hell," the soldier replied bluntly.

The two deputies stared at him, studying his face, his expression, his eyes.

Proudfoot was impressed by the physical appearance of the man who sat across from him. They had been too busy for him to study the one-man army. He looked even larger than the six foot three his wife had told him Belasko was. If he weighed two hundred pounds, it was all muscle and toughened sinew.

The man was larger than life. The deputy had

met many gunmen, but none with the self-confident expression, the cold, piercing eyes Belasko possessed. He looked like someone who had taken care of himself and others for a very long time.

"You really mean it, don't you? About not packing up and going home."

Bolan nodded.

"You're crazy. I hate watching someone commit suicide."

"Nobody invited you to join up. I work alone."

The two deputies exchanged looks.

"That's a shame," Tallchief commented. "You need a couple of trained fighters who can steer you to the right contacts, get you to the right places."

Tallchief took over the conversation. "For instance, do you know where Marty Comer's studio is?"

"I've got a general idea. But no, I don't have an exact location," Bolan admitted.

"We're going with you."

"No. Like it or not, the two of you are cops, not government agents."

"We could resign," Proudfoot suggested.

"You're more valuable doing what you've been doing. And both of you have families."

"We talked it over with them before we came here," Tallchief revealed. "We've got almost two hundred years of hate, prejudice and murder to make up for. Comer and his fans are exactly like the men who made our ancestors walk across the country to Oklahoma. And let more than four thousand of them die on the journey."

The Executioner couldn't be burdened with the responsibility of other lives but when he studied the deputies' faces, he knew there was no talking them out of joining him. Even if he refused, he knew he had planted the seed in their minds of going all the way in standing up to racist killers.

"Let me put it more bluntly," Proudfoot said. "Whether or not you want us as part of your team, we're going to be there."

Bolan knew there was no point in arguing. Or time.

"Just keep out of my way," he ordered.

"You'll know we're there when the hate mongers start dying."

The Executioner shrugged. "It'll take more power than you two have got in your six-shooters."

"We salvaged some MAC-10s and M-16s, as well as ammo for them, before we hauled your ass up here," Tallchief answered.

"Know how to use them?"

The deputies nodded. "We used M-16s in the Middle East. And as far as the MAC-10s go, we trained at the Secret Service range when we signed on as deputies," Proudfoot stated. "As you know, the White House detail of the Secret Service had exclusive use of the Ingrams until they switched to Uzi SMGs.

THE MAN behind the large desk signaled Hal Brognola to take a seat in one of the pair of easy chairs facing him.

"I got a call from Senator Harvey McCutcheon," the President said.

"What did he want?"

"Nothing good, Hal. He threatened to call a public hearing of his subcommittee to investigate whether the government was responsible for the deaths of members of the Carolina Militia."

Brognola smiled. It wasn't often that the head of the Stony Man Farm complex displayed emotion.

"I guess my man is starting to make waves," he commented. "And I have to wonder why McCutcheon is putting up a stink."

"Next time you talk to your man, suggest he ease off on the amount of damage he does."

"It doesn't work that way, Mr. President. With Striker, it's all or nothing. If you want him to stop, I can try to convince him to walk away from the problem. But you know that Mack Bolan believes in every cause he undertakes, and he never uses more violence than he feels is necessary."

The President did some thinking.

"Let Striker continue. I have enough on the good senator to shut him up for a while."

BECAUSE THE DEPUTIES knew the area intimately, Bolan had asked Proudfoot to drive. The Executioner sat next to him, while Frank Tallchief was behind him.

Bolan studied the wooded dirt road as they drove along.

"Pull over," he ordered suddenly. Surprised at the harshness in his voice, Proudfoot pulled off the road and stopped the vehicle, then turned to Bolan.

"Something wrong?"

The soldier tried to listen past the usual night sounds. Nothing. Was it fatigue? he wondered.

Reaching for the canvas bag, he took out the M-16 A-2 he had packed and a handful of clips, which he shoved into the pockets of the combat vest. Checking the carbine's clip, he snapped in a fresh magazine and jacked the first round into the chamber. Then he loaded an incendiary grenade into the M-203 launcher mounted beneath the powerful rifle's barrel.

Seemingly satisfied, Bolan started to rise, then changed his mind and reached into the bag again. As he brought out a long tube, Proudfoot, who'd been watching him, recognized the weapon.

"Why on earth would you need a LAW right now?"

"I might not," Bolan replied, slinging the antitank rocket over a shoulder. "But then again, who knows." He nodded toward the road. "Let's get going."

As Proudfoot resumed driving, the soldier could feel the tension radiating from the two deputies.

"It might be nothing," he said, trying to reassure his companions, "but if there is an attack, follow my orders pronto. Every minute you delay could cost us our—"

The rest of his sentence was punctuated by automatic fire pouring like a sudden rainstorm from both sides of the road.

"Get this car off the road and into the woods," he shouted, grabbing the M-16 A-2 combo.

CHAPTER NINETEEN

Without hesitation, Proudfoot spun the steering wheel hard and plunged into an open space in the bushes. The Jeep bucked as it bounced on the uneven forest ground.

Frank Tallchief managed to hold onto the rear seat.

"Stop," Bolan shouted.

Stomping on the brakes, Proudfoot managed to stop the vehicle, causing it to stall as he did.

"Spread out," Bolan ordered the pair sharply. "One of you go to the right and the other to the left."

Gripping their assault rifles, the deputies moved silently into the woods.

Bolan pushed his way into the thick brush and moved toward the source of the gunfire. Two fatigue-clad assailants had their backs turned to him.

The sound of a small branch breaking made them spin around, their Calico subguns up and ready. At the sight of the Executioner, the pair started to squeeze their triggers.

Bolan had anticipated their actions. Whirling to the left like a fullback avoiding a tackler, he loosed a burst of 5.56 mm man slayers from his M-16 at the closer of the pair. The rounds carved a path through the assassin's neck and up into his brain.

The second assassin recovered quickly from the shock of seeing his cohort torn apart, and hastily emptied his magazine of 5.56 mm ammo at where Bolan had been standing. But the Executioner had twisted out of the way, and the rounds from the gunman's SMG chopped chunks of wood from the trunk of a tree behind him.

While the hit man tried to force a fresh magazine into his weapon, Bolan swept his carbine in a left-to-right path across the midsection of the second attacker. Screaming curses, the hit man dropped his SMG and tried desperately to stop his intestines from spilling onto the ground.

Looking down at the huge cavity where his stomach and digestive organs had been minutes earlier, the dying fighter saw the blood from his body wash over his hands, then abruptly sat down as death claimed him.

SCANNING THE NEARBY WOODS for additional hidden enemies, Bolan sensed the presence of a large force on both sides of the highway. He knew he could stand and fight, but he had a more important task—confronting the racist talk-show host.

It was time to retreat. He whistled loudly, and the two deputies emerged from behind a tree.

"What's up?" Tallchief asked.

"Time to leave and get to Comer's place."

As they approached the Jeep, Bolan stopped. "Get the car started. I'll be there in a minute."

The men started to argue with him, then changed their minds when they saw the look on the soldier's face that brooked no argument.

THE SOLDIER LISTENED for a moment, then focused carefully through the sight mounted on the left and adjusted the setting. Squeezing the trigger on the M-203 grenade launcher, he watched as the missile traveled above the treetops. Then he turned and ran for the military vehicle.

Getting behind the wheel of the vehicle, Billy Proudfoot waited until Bolan got in, then started the engine and floored the gas pedal.

As the Jeep raced through the woods in the direction of the paved highway, the three men could hear the loud explosions of ammo set off by the grenade the Executioner had delivered.

"That takes care of that group," Billy commented in a calmer voice.

"We're not there yet," the soldier warned.

As if his words had been a prophecy, an armored personnel carrier lumbered out of the woods in front of them.

Sitting above the driver in a small swivel seat, a fatigue-clad man squinted carefully through the sight of the 5-56 mm AK-47 assault rifle.

"Weave!" Bolan shouted.

The driver swerved the Jeep into a series of half figure-eights.

A steady stream of angry hornets streamed from the mounted machine gun, missing the Jeep and its occupants by scant inches.

"The gunner's getting too accurate. Into the woods!"

"Can't we outrun him?"

"Not with the range of that machine gun, and we don't know what other kind of weapons they're carrying."

Proudfoot drove the Jeep over the shoulder and headed for a clearing in the underbrush.

Bolan jumped from the vehicle before it stopped. "I'll be back," he promised.

MAJOR AARON LOCKSLEY opened the door of the APC and stared at the gunner.

"Why did you stop firing?"

"They ran into the forest, Major," the gunner explained.

"Follow them," the official commanded.

He turned to a corporal. "Have we heard from the rest of the force?"

"A few minutes ago, sir. They reached the target area and are about to enter. They calculate it will take ten minutes to plant the explosives," the corporal replied. "They'll meet us at the rendezvous in twenty minutes."

Locksley nodded. As usual, the information from Washington, D.C., was accurate. The President's mercenary was here. The major didn't know who the others were, but assumed they were hired gunmen.

Everything was on schedule. The other part of the military exercise was moving ahead as planned. Now it was up to him to make certain this part was, too.

Then he could return the APC to the local depot from which it had been taken.

As the driver spun the wheel of the armored vehicle, the major reached down and picked up an MM-1 multiround projectile launcher. Checking the twelve missiles in the awkward-looking weapon, he commented, "We'll burn them out with these incendiary grenades, or they can stay hidden and roast to death."

Ahead of him, he could see the faint outline of the Jeep hiding behind some hardwood trees twenty yards in front of them.

"Stop here," he ordered, and got out when the carrier came to a halt. "Maintain a stream of gunfire on the Jeep."

The weight of the bulky MM-1 made the major stoop slightly. It had been a long time since he'd last fired a grenade launcher.

He leaned against the personnel carrier and began to unleash a steady stream of incendiaries. Trees and bushes ignited, sending clouds of smoke skyward. The frightened sounds of birds fleeing the area echoed in the sky.

"The general will be pleased," he exclaimed proudly.

It was the last thing he or his men ever said.

BOLAN HAD SLIPPED behind the trees until he had a clear view of the APC. He checked to make sure neither of the deputies was in front of him.

Reassured by the distant sound of high-powered rounds, he slipped the LAW 80 from his shoulder and pulled the safety pin. The end caps fell away, and the weapon telescoped another six inches while it armed itself.

The nearly three-foot-long shoulder-held missile launcher carried a 94 mm round with a hollowpoint nose, shaped like a small teacup.

Sighting through the eyepiece that moved into position on top of the launcher, the Executioner saw the flames spitting up as each of the enemy's launched grenades made contact with a tree or the packed dirt.

Focusing on the armored personnel carrier, he pulled the trigger. The missile raced out of the tube at a speed of almost five hundred feet per second and easily cut a hole through the APC as if it were made of paper.

The missile exploded with the deafening sound of thunder, tearing the armored vehicle in two. Molten bits of metal from the warhead and flames shot back at him, scorching trees in their path.

Over the exploding ammo, Bolan could hear muffled screams as superheated chunks of metal and flame consumed the men in and around the

APC. The smell of burning flesh fouled the air, making him feel slightly nauseous.

He waited for the intense heat to dissipate, then worked his way back to where the Jeep was parked.

Proudfoot was waiting for him, crouching on the floor of the vehicle. He started to point the M-16 at him, then lowered it when he realized it was Bolan.

Tallchief joined him. "Next time, we go with you," he snapped.

"I felt like a helpless bystander watching a war being fought," Proudfoot said.

Getting into the Jeep, Bolan pointed to the wheel. "Drive. I'm too beat to argue."

The enemy had tossed another set of assassins into the area, and the Executioner had managed to survive the attack. If Brognola failed to plug the leak, next time he might not be so lucky.

CHAPTER TWENTY

Marty Comer thought he had the world by its tail. He'd been on a roll for almost four years. And if the money kept pouring in from sponsors and backers, he'd be worth more than a million dollars by the end of the year.

All neatly deposited in safe-deposit boxes around the country.

And he had eight of the local sheriff's toughest deputies on his payroll as bodyguards.

Not bad for a Kentucky coal miner's kid, he thought as he got ready to deliver his daily message of hate and civil disobedience. Colonel Timmons had sent a whole platoon of former antiinsurgent specialists to check out the studio, headed up a by mean-faced lieutenant, and make sure nobody got to him. He waited in the reception room while they went over his studio with a fine-tooth comb.

The only thing that was really bugging him at this moment was the slaughter in the Smoky Mountains. Ever since he had started a campaign to muzzle federal agents from the FBI, DEA and ATF, the administration had handled him with kid gloves.

Now they had to have decided to come back with a vengeance.

They were violent enough with the weekend soldiers up in the national park. According to reports his contacts had passed along to him, they were even more violent when they confronted the White Aryan Resistance bikers.

He hated losing the two groups. They had paid him plenty to promote their causes. But their murders provided enough ammunition for at least six broadcasts.

Before he was done, Congress would be forced to start hearings on why the administration's gunmen had abused their power and killed innocent people. He would make sure the deck was stacked so that his listeners would hear it that way.

And he knew he could count on Senator McCutcheon to play the two mass murders for every bit of free publicity he could get. He knew the senator well. McCutcheon was more than a conservative. He had a private agenda that would elect his kind of people to positions of power and guarantee that issues such as excessive and unwarranted taxation, as well as a Communist-backed attempt to have refugees deplete the financial resources of the United States, were brought to the table.

The lieutenant in charge of the team led his men out of the studio.

"It's ready for you to get back and do your broadcast," the Army officer reported. "We'll be hanging around outside to make sure no one tries to get inside."

"I asked the deputies on my payroll to put themselves under your command. They're tough, and they know how to use weapons."

"Hopefully, we won't need them. But the more guns we have, the safer you are."

Comer nodded gratefully, then glanced at his watch. No more thinking. The broadcast started in twenty minutes. As glib as he knew he was, he needed a few minutes to put his thoughts together.

The engineer had moved into the equipment-filled room next to his. Comer could see Harry Michaels through the thick glass window. Their communication was limited by the fact that they could only speak to each other using their microphones.

"Morning, Marty," Michaels said cheerfully.

"Ready to go?" Comer asked.

"Tape's racked up, and I tied us in to our network of stations. They've got their lines open. I'll signal you when we're on the air."

The broadcaster arranged his notes on a music stand and sprayed his throat with a special medication his doctor had given him.

He had been hearing a slight ticking noise from the microphone, and it was starting to bother him. A half-million dollars' worth of equipment in the studio he had built, and it developed a strange noise.

He started to mention the sound to Michaels, then decided to call his wife. Maybe this time she'd wish him luck. She never had before, but there was always a first time.

He lifted the phone and punched in the number. He'd forgotten to tell her he was flying to Washington to meet with the senator and then with the Pentagon contact. Both had collected contributions to keep his broadcasts on the air.

The ticking noise continued. Comer started to get mad. He slammed the phone down onto its cradle and flipped the switch that allowed him to talk to his engineer.

The ticking seemed to be getting louder. The

broadcaster started to get concerned that the noise might interfere with his show.

"Harry, there's a weird noise coming from my broadcast console. What do you think it is?"

"I'll figure it out later. I can't hear it in my headphones, so it's strictly coming from something in your studio."

The engineer stopped and said something into his microphone, then opened the line between Comer and him.

"You're on the air, Marty."

"This is Martin Comer," the broadcaster said in a silken tone. "Today I want to talk about heroes who were murdered by a professional assassin hired by the administration.

"His name is—"

He never finished the sentence. The ticking had become increasingly louder until it erupted into a ear-shattering explosion that tore parts of his body from his torso and spattered the shattered window separating his studio from the control room with his blood.

As BOLAN DROVE the Jeep along Route 29, Frank Tallchief filled him in on the kind of people he'd find in Spring River.

"The people who live here are just like Comer.

That's why the racist skunk built his studio there. They've got a policy of letting only White Aryans buy or rent here, and the sheriff and his men are just like everybody else there. No minorities permitted. Blacks, Jews, Asians and Indians have a tough time when they try to drive through Spring River. Sometimes the deputies invent laws on the spot and make the minorities passing through pay a just-created fine.''

"Great town to raise kids," Bolan observed.

"If you want them to grow up to become bigots," Proudfoot replied.

Physically, Spring River reminded the soldier of a hundred small towns he'd visited. A handful of run-down retail stores, five bars and two gas stations made up the commercial part of the community. All of them bordered the two-lane highway.

The residents lived on farms or small houses as far from Route 29 as they could.

"Nearest place to do any real shopping or get medical help is over in Waynesville," Tallchief commented as he searched the streets that bordered the highway for signs of life. "Notice there isn't anybody on the street. Their kids are in school in that small brick building up in the hills."

He pointed to an ancient-looking structure.

"Where are the adults?" Bolan asked.

"The grown-ups like to keep to themselves," the deputy stated. "Unless they're going to church on Sunday, or a gathering of one of the branches of some antigovernment or racist group."

A new one-story building stood on the right, just ahead of them. Bolan asked about it.

"Combination town hall, sheriff's headquarters, fire house and jail."

Before they could continue their conversation, the trio heard an explosion roughly a mile from where the two deputies said Comer's studio was located.

"Any munitions warehouses in town?" Bolan asked.

"If there are any, they're well hidden from detection," Tallchief stated. "I haven't been here many times, but I'd swear it came from someplace near Comer's building."

"Then either some explosives he was storing were set off or somebody got to him before we did," the Executioner growled.

"Good riddance," Proudfoot said. "He's deserved to die for a long time."

"Yeah," Bolan agreed, "but now we can't ask

him about the powerful backers he bragged about on his broadcasts.''

''I never thought of that,'' Tallchief said apologetically.

''Unless it was an accident, you can bet somebody did,'' Bolan replied.

Something else was strange about the explosion—nobody had come to investigate, at least not that he could see.

The Executioner formed a strategy as they moved closer to the building. The roof looked sturdy enough to support one or two men.

He pulled the Jeep off the road and turned toward the deputies. ''Let's get our gear together and move in.''

While the two deputies filled their denim jacket pockets with magazines of ammo and shouldered their M-16s and MAC-10s, Bolan filled his shoulder holster with the silenced 9 mm Baretta 93-R, then strapped the stiff sheath that held the Applegate-Fairbairn blade to his left forearm.

Slipping a webbed combat belt around his waist, he grabbed the holster that cradled the massive Israeli-made .44 Magnum Desert Eagle and hooked a half-dozen frag and incendiary grenades into the metal-rimmed eyelets.

Extra magazines for the two handguns, as well as for the M-16 and Uzi SMG he planned to carry into combat, easily slid into the pockets of the combat vest he donned.

Because the majority of battle would be close combat, Bolan opted to take the Uzi submachine gun, as well as the more powerful Colt carbine.

In the soldier's estimation, the Uzi was a solid fighting tool. The Israeli-manufactured SMG weighed less than eight pounds and was compact. Each magazine clipped into its grip held twenty-five rounds of high-velocity ammo, and the weapon could be fired one-handed when necessary. The weapon's 9 mm Parabellum rounds hurtled out of the barrel at the rate of six hundred rounds a minute, with a velocity of 1,250 feet per second, and changing magazines took seconds—vital features when a soldier or lawman depended on his weapon to help him stay alive.

Bolan turned to the pair of lawmen.

"Ready? Billy, I want you on the roof. Frank, check around the perimeter of the studio building for hidden gunners." He looked at the stocky man. "Don't try to take them on by yourself." He turned to Proudfoot. "Same goes for you.

"A couple of loud whistles will get me to your side the minute I hear them."

The deputies nodded.

"Okay, we'll move in closer as a team, then split up."

CHAPTER TWENTY-ONE

Bert Holiday clicked off on the cellular phone he was holding and whistled for the others to listen.

Speaking softly, the mercenary warned, "They should be showing up any minute. One of our lookouts spotted a Jeep driving on Route 29 into town."

Holiday was the leader of the squad sent by Colonel Timmons. Head of a unit operating undercover in Guatemala until he and his platoon-sized team of mercenaries were recalled the previous year, Holiday had a score to settle with the man who called himself Mike Belasko.

Felipe DeSantos, the man Belasko killed at the Asheville airport, had been on Holiday's Central American team. The mercenary leader had prided himself on never having lost one of his men to a bullet or knife.

As they listened, the ten men in combat fatigues gripped their weapons, eager to engage the enemy. Each carried an M-16 A-2 with an M-203 grenade launcher mounted beneath the barrel. Their combat vests were filled with full magazines for the combat rifle, and clipped to metal loops on the outside of the garment were fragmentation grenades.

Holiday looked around and asked a question. "Who's got the C-4?"

One of his men raised his hand.

"You remember to bring a wireless detonator?"

"That's what you asked for," the merc specialist announced. "I tested it. It works."

"Good. Plant it in the front entrance, then join me." He turned to the others. "Two of you on the roof. The rest of you spread out and find convenient hiding places in here.

"And," he added in a chilling tone, "check your weapons. Your rifle hangs up, and you're dead. If this Belasko doesn't take you out, I will."

Five men in denim or khaki work clothes watched as the mercs scattered. One of them approached Holiday.

"What about us? The sheriff said we should give you a hand."

The mercenary team leader hated amateurs, and

the five deputies weren't up to the standard of his team. He was about to send them back to the local headquarters, then decided they might come in handy if they didn't get in the way of his men.

"You men hide in the bushes outside the building. Shoot anyone going in or anyone coming out who doesn't look familiar."

One of the deputies fondled his Konzak combat shotgun. The others gripped a variety of weapons: 9 mm Tec-9 and .45-caliber MAC-10 subguns.

One of them cradled a 12-gauge Street Sweeper. The pug-ugly weapon looked like a submachine gun, but fired 12-gauge shotgun loads at a rapid rate. Reloading was simple.

The weapon had been tested by street gangs across the country, specifically when they intended to wipe out a rival group.

Holiday glanced at the shotgun.

"Nice weapon," he commented, cynicism filling his voice. "Just remember that we're killing men, not grizzly bears."

BOLAN WANTED to make sure Marty Comer was dead. If he wasn't, the soldier had every intention of rescuing him.

Years of combat experience had taught him

how to move in on a target without making noise. Now was no exception.

Bolan approached the windows on the street side of the building and peered inside. Despite the darkness and dust, he could see the pile of rubble in the center of the interior. Comer, he decided, had to be under it.

Dead.

The Executioner hoped that all of his files hadn't been destroyed in the explosion. Perhaps he could get a clue to the broadcaster's high-level backers from them.

He started to enter the building, then spotted shadows inside dart behind the rubble. Now he knew he was facing an ambush. How many men and who had sent them—those were unknown facts.

There was an expedient solution.

Unclipping a delay frag grenade from his vest, he loaded it onto the launcher, then aimed toward the pile of rubble and pulled back on the trigger.

There was a sudden flash of light and a wave of extreme heat as the grenade exploded. Bolan heard pitiful screams and moans from across the room. Even though he couldn't determine how many had been waiting to ambush him inside, he knew that he hadn't missed the target.

Flames started to creep across paneled walls. The Executioner shouldered the M-16 while he waited for the flames to die down. Holding his Uzi in front of him, he moved carefully into the building.

A hint of movement drew Bolan's attention, and he did a forward flip out of the path of a spray of Parabellum lead from a Tec-9. Twisting, he clicked his weapon to autofire and stunned the merc with a barrage of flesh seekers.

Despite his wounds, the fatigue-clad killer started to curse as he forced himself to his feet.

Bolan dropped the now empty Uzi, jerked the Desert Eagle from its holster and pumped three slugs of .44 Magnum lead at the enemy gunner.

Finally, the enraged hardman shoved his huge hands in front of him and tried to grab Bolan, but he slipped in a puddle of his own blood and gore. He collapsed to the floor, succumbing to his wounds.

The Executioner kicked the weapon away from the body, then squatted and felt the artery in the attacker's neck for a pulse.

There was none.

Bolan glanced at the destruction all around him. Shattered bricks and chunks of plaster covered the center of the building. Whatever records Comer

kept had been demolished in the fire that had to
have followed the explosion.

Searching through the ruins, the Executioner
found two bodies. One had been crushed by the
heavy broadcasting equipment under which he
was buried. Bolan suspected he was the engineer,
not Marty Comer. The second body was dressed
in obviously expensive casual clothes. His hand
still grasped sheets of typewritten pages.

The soldier eased the script from the dead
man's hand and glanced at it. The pages were
filled with words of hate. There was a demand
that the radio audience rise up against a government that was trying to destroy what it called
"real Americans."

There was no pity in Bolan's eyes as he hol-
stered the Desert Eagle and searched through
Comer's pockets. The wallet he found was filled
with cash and credit cards, and it contained a
scrap of paper, burned at the edges from the
flames of explosion. It had a telephone number
and the name B. Scott, as well as the words, "Delivery urgent. IRS attacks as soon as he gets
guns."

Bolan pocketed the paper. He'd ask Brognola
to check it out when he called in his report.

Then he thought of something. Comer rarely

traveled, yet kept in touch with his contacts and backers. How?

A shattered telephone on the floor gave him the simple answer.

By telephone.

Brognola had the clout to check out incoming and outgoing calls. This should be a breeze for the big Fed.

The sounds of shoes crunching broken glass behind him snapped Bolan back to the present. Without knowing how many men were in the building with him, the soldier dived for the cover of a massive metal desk that had been turned on its side by the blast.

Without pausing, he pulled the silenced Beretta 93-R from shoulder leather as he heard 9 mm lead denting the thick metal that was his shield.

Glancing out from an edge of the desk, he saw a crew-cut merc in fatigues and a denim-garbed deputy, still wearing the badge of office on his work shirt. Both held micro-Uzi autopistols.

The Executioner waited until the pair emptied the magazines in their deadly weapons. Then, as they raced to change clips, Bolan pointed the Beretta at the closer of the two and fired two 9 mm slugs.

As the missiles carved into the hit man's chest,

the cavity they caused revealed the shattered blood vessels and bones inside. Bolan didn't wait for the second assailant to pull the trigger of his autopistol. He did a shoulder roll into a pile of rubble on his right before the second hit man could get off the first shot. Then, from his belly-down position, he drilled two rounds between the thug's eyes.

Blood and bits of shredded brain exploded into the air as the bullet tore a large hole in the man's skull.

With caution, Bolan moved to the bodies and kicked their weapons away from their still hands. There was something strange about the body clad in fatigues, and it wasn't just his military haircut.

The soldier searched through the fatigue pockets for some identification. Nothing. The dead man was obviously a professional.

Then instinct took over. Bolan tore open the fatigue jacket, and there it was. A military identification tag, hanging from a beaded chain. He tore it from the corpse and read the metal-stamped words: "First Lieutenant Lair Miles. Special Forces."

A flood of questions raced through the Executioner's mind.

Who was Miles, and who had sent him?

Bolan had already collected a full day's work for Brognola's specialists at Stony Man Farm. The answers might give him a clue to who was behind the racist and antigovernment groups.

And why.

A series of explosions outside the building drew his attention. It was time to check in with Proudfoot and Tallchief.

BILLY PROUDFOOT WRAPPED his arm around an exhaust pipe and helped pull his heavier comrade to the roof of the single-storied structure. Three men in military fatigues had made their last stand on the ground below them. To Bolan, the shattered bodies were evidence enough that the Native American deputies knew how to fight.

Proudfoot waved down to Bolan, then checked his M-16. His clip was nearly empty. He slammed home a fresh one and lay spread-eagle on the roof. Tallchief pulled himself up beside him, his assault weapon hanging from his neck on its strap.

They could see bodies on the ground, and more than four or five men firing MAC-10s as they charged at the camouflage-clad soldier on the ground.

"Party time," Proudfoot yelled.

Tallchief pushed the butt of his M-16 into his

shoulder and lined up the sights. "Ready when you are."

Using the parapet of the building as a rest for their combat carbines, the deputies carefully lined up the attackers in their sights.

It had been obvious to Bolan that the pair on the roof knew what they were doing when they selected the Colt rifle as their weapon of choice. Not only was the M-16 A-2 capable of pouring 800 rounds of high-velocity 5.56 mm ammo per minute at a muzzle velocity of 1000 meters per second with virtually no jamming, but the launcher made it possible to hurtle a 40 mm grenade accurately as far as 350 meters.

The pair poured a volley of lead on the rapidly approaching hired professionals, taking three men out of the play.

The Executioner reached to his belt and yanked a frag grenade free, then armed and lobbed the metal oval downfield.

As he watched, the 40 mm missile spiraled toward four hit men who chose to hide in a small olive-drab-colored truck.

Chunks of exploding metal gouged flesh from two of the attackers. Injured severely, the pair still managed to exit their burning vehicle and run into the one-story brick building.

"My turn," Proudfoot yelled, and tossed a frag grenade into the building through a hole in the roof. The deputies and Bolan could hear the muffled sound of the missile erupting inside, and the screams of men peppered by overheated slivers of metal tearing into their bodies.

A trio of attackers who had been hiding, waiting their turn to prove their skill as front line combatants, looked around at the dead and started to run for a small military truck.

The two young deputies slid to the edge of the roof and let themselves drop to the ground.

Proudfoot checked with Bolan. "You want us to bring them back alive?"

The soldier nodded. "They might have some information."

The two men jumped into the Jeep and took off after the retreating professional hit men, yelling as they pursued them, while the Executioner took a breather and watched.

He spotted a second Army truck parked beside the shattered building. It was time to get rid of anyone who might be left.

A small brick of C-4 bulged one of his pants pockets. From the same pocket, he took a miniaturized detonator and timer. He slid under the truck and pressed the clump of plastic explosive to the gas tank. After setting the timer for ten minutes, the soldier started to slide out. He stopped abruptly when he spied two pairs of military jump boots standing on the right side of the truck.

Obviously, they hadn't detected his presence.

One of the two men started to speak.

"Have you seen the lieutenant?"

"No," came the answer, "but I'm not waiting for him to show up."

"We can get our asses in a sling if we leave him behind," the first man warned.

"I'm thinking of some bullshit to hand the colonel when we get back."

"It better be good," the first man commented, sounding worried. "You've seen how guys who don't follow orders get treated."

"Yeah," the other voice replied. "They get dead. But that isn't going to happen to us. You gather up anybody still alive and let's get out of this burg. I'll get the truck going and start thinking about a good excuse."

Bolan waited for the feet to disappear. He could hear one pair crunching crushed rock as the man ran to search for whoever was left. The second guy climbed into the truck cab and started the engine.

The Executioner slid out the other side and hid behind some bushes. Staring at the cruel face behind the steering wheel, he was tempted to turn him into a corpse with the Beretta 93-R he was gripping in his right hand. But he changed his mind when he saw five men sprinting toward the truck. He knew the plastic explosive would take care of what was left of the Army platoon.

One of the men yelled a question.

"What about the local cops? Do we take them with us?"

"No way," the driver yelled back. "They're on their own."

The men jumped into the back of the truck, and the driver took off down the highway.

And to his appointment with the Devil.

Only a handful of local cops remained alive. Rogue cops, Bolan reminded himself.

And the men in the truck the deputies were chasing.

The Executioner started to search the area for the local bodyguards, then saw a Chevrolet Camaro racing across the unpaved field next to the shattered studio building. He could see the three men in it, and their badges.

From the terror painted across their faces, the

soldier suspected they wouldn't stop running until they were halfway across the state.

There was no point wasting time thinking about them. He had a couple of lawmen to wait for, a call to make to Stony Man Farm and a war that was ready to turn into a holocaust.

At least for the killers who had decided to start it.

CHAPTER TWENTY-TWO

Leaning on the edge of the desk in the secret room, the lanky middle-aged man listened to what the caller had to say, then slammed the telephone on its cradle. He was furious at Marty Comer for getting killed, and at the White Aryan Resistance biker gang that was supposed to deliver a truck-load of guns, ammunition, rockets and launchers, several cases of grenades, a case of C-4 plastic explosive along with detonators and timers.

It wasn't that the Tax Resisters' Alliance didn't have weapons and explosives. There was a cache stored behind a false wall in the barn that backed on the meeting room.

Byron Scott believed they needed more to sell to the new members they hoped to attract after they eliminated the IRS offices.

The radio-talk-show host had promised the

shipment would arrive before dark when Scott and he spoke early that morning.

Now the secret meeting room was filled with members. The leader of the TAR had worked hard for this moment for a lot of years. Tax Liberation Day was supposed to happen three days from now.

In his mind, the chiropractor-turned-part-time-farmer could see the confusion and terror on the faces of those who collected taxes for the government, and those who had agreed to pay.

Explosives would detonate in the IRS regional office in Raleigh. Where the C-4 didn't demolish the tax office, the attackers would launch HEAT rockets through the shattered doors and windows. In the confusion, all of his men would escape. The latex masks he would provide them with would hide their identities.

The administration would get what it deserved—a lot of terrified and angry voters who didn't trust anyone.

Byron Scott turned to the others and told them what he had just learned.

"Who did it?" asked Jimmy Joe Marker.

"Some mercenary named Belasko—or something like that—hired by the President to wipe us out. The guy on the other end of the line said he might be coming here.''

Scott didn't explain that the caller was a Pentagon officer.

The only woman in the room, LuAnn Rankin, voiced her disgust.

''Forget this Belasko. We've got bigger problems. We got Tax Liberation Day coming up and we haven't got the stuff we need to tell people that the days of slamming them with outrageous taxes are over,'' the slim, dark-haired woman complained.

Everyone in the room knew Rankin's history. Her husband had a small business. They hadn't paid the taxes the IRS had levied, so the government had foreclosed on their new house.

In the melee that followed, her husband, Link, had grabbed a loaded 12-gauge shotgun.

The leader of the IRS contingent had started to reach in his inner jacket pocket for the official foreclosure permit. Link, already at the edge of panic, had watched the hand go inside the jacket and fired twice at the IRS man, killing him.

The rest of the government team had escaped in the confusion and called for assistance from the local FBI office. By the time the federal team had arrived, Link had ordered LuAnn out of the house and barricaded the doors.

By the time the siege was over, Link had killed two FBI men and wounded two more. Pulling back a safe distance, the federal agents made a decision to stop the battle.

From inside the truck, one of them had brought a rocket launcher. The clumsy-looking tubular device had sights on top. The agent had steadied himself and released the missile. It tore through the front door as if it were made of paper, then the walls of their house had shattered in every direction.

When it was over, the paramedics brought out the parts of Link's body they could find.

The next day, rather than wasting her time mourning Link's death, LuAnn Rankin had started a chapter of the Tax Resisters' Alliance.

"What we need are explosives and rockets," she announced.

"You can't go into some retail store and buy rockets," one of the men commented cynically.

"We can get explosives," she countered.

"How?" another man asked. "We can't show proof that we own a construction company, so something like that is out."

Scott saw an opportunity to save the plan.

"We can steal them," he told the others. "There's a place that sells supplies to contractors. We can go in and check whether they carry explosives."

"What about rockets?" someone asked.

Scott remembered Marty Comer telling him to call a Colonel Timmons at the Pentagon if he ever needed help.

"Let me think about it. I might have a solution."

"Either you do," Rankin snapped, angrily, "or we call off Tax Liberation Day. And I won't do that, if I have to go by myself to the IRS office."

Byron Scott knew the woman was serious. And if she was caught, nobody in the room would be safe from retaliation by federal agents.

Scott excused himself and dialed the number in Washington, D.C., Comer had given him.

A voice on the other end answered, "Timmons."

Scott introduced himself.

"He mentioned you and your group to me."

"The...supplies we ordered were destroyed on their way."

Timmons interrupted. "I know. I got the report."

Quickly, Scott outlined his group's plans.

THE COLONEL LEANED BACK in his chair and weighed the effect attacks on an IRS office would have on the public. Many would be horrified at the number of people killed, but many would understand that being overtaxed drove the attackers to their desperate acts.

"I can get them to you in twenty-four hours. I'll call you back in two hours with instructions on where to find them."

Timmons's secretary walked into his office.

"I'm sorry. I didn't know you were on the phone, Colonel," she commented.

"I am, Mary Sue. But we'll be done in a few minutes and I'll buzz you."

He waited for the young woman to walk out of his office and close the door behind her.

He thought of a way he could get the Tax Resisters' Alliance members to kill Mack Bolan.

"There is a man who calls himself Mike Belasko."

"Never heard of him," Scott replied.

"In exchange for the supplies I'll have delivered to your barn, I want you to kill him."

"You sure he's heading this way?"

Timmons thought of the information General Lawrence's White House contact had passed along to him.

"I'm positive."

The contact was the President's personal secretary, Lillian Henshaw. The general and she had been discreet lovers for many years, long before General Lawrence's wife and daughter had been killed.

It was Lawrence who had encouraged her to take the high-level position when the President had offered it to her.

"I want to stay here in the Pentagon where you are," she had pleaded.

"Somehow we'll find the time to be together," the general had promised.

With that assurance, Lillian accepted the offer. After she had made the move, the general had confided in Timmons.

"For the first time, I feel really free."

"She would be useful in feeding us information on the President's plans for the military."

Lawrence had smiled. "Good thinking, Colonel. I'll remember that when I'm in bed with her."

"You can count on us," Scott promised. "And those weapons will help drive out the Washington dictators."

Timmons wanted to laugh. All of this talk about cleansing the country. He knew the general too well. Lawrence had only one goal, and that was getting himself elected President.

With civil unrest on the rise, someone like a general with his record had a better than even chance of getting elected.

General Eisenhower did it in the fifties. Why not him now?

THE HEAD OF Stony Man Farm had put his best man on the two questions the Executioner had posed to him: Who was B. Scott, and who was the lieutenant Bolan had killed at the studio?

He had to wait until the soldier called him to give him the answers. That evening, his personal security phone rang. Mack Bolan was on the other end of the line.

He was calling from a small motel forty miles outside Spring River.

Brognola kept his report brief. "B. Scott is Byron Scott, a retired chiropractor. He lives on a farm in Lynchville, a small town outside of Birmingham, Alabama. He's had a personal feud with the Internal Revenue Service for years. He refuses to pay taxes. Scott claims the government gets enough from the taxes they charge businesses for things he buys.

"He's obsessed with the idea of shutting down

the IRS. The FBI and IRS could deal with the problem if it was just him, but he's traveled around the country blaming the IRS for all of his problems. And he's pulled together more than a hundred nuts from several states into a group that calls itself the Tax Resisters' Alliance. They seem to agree with his solution—kill the tax people and blow up their offices.

"They get together at least once or twice a year, usually around this time, to egg each other on about finally taking action. Scott's farm in the hills is where they usually meet."

Bolan had been making notes as he listened.

"What about the Army lieutenant?" he asked.

"We don't have a real answer to why he was there. Not yet," Brognola admitted. "All we know is his name and something of his background. Lair Miles has been in the military for almost twenty years. He joined as an enlisted man, served during Desert Storm and won medals for combat action, then got a field promotion to lieutenant."

"Anything about his politics or personal beliefs?" Bolan asked.

"If he had any personal beliefs, he never shared them with anybody else. As far as politics is concerned, he never voiced an opinion on any candidates," the big Fed replied.

"I wonder who sent him to Marty Comer's studio?"

"All his captain knew was that Miles was called into a Colonel Gregory Timmons's office in the Pentagon and took an emergency leave immediately afterward."

"Timmons?"

"He's part of the Special Services Group in the Pentagon. Timmons has a long history of running 'special services.' During Vietnam and Desert Storm, he was responsible for hiring mercenaries and unearthing local dissidents. He'd arm and train them to carry out special missions for the military."

The report on Timmons caught the soldier's interest. "Who does Timmons report to?"

"A general named Mark Lawrence," Brognola replied.

The Executioner decided to put that aside for the moment. There was a more pressing problem that required his attention.

He asked for directions to Scott's farm in Lynchville.

CHAPTER TWENTY-THREE

Captain Leslie Blake had served under Colonel Gregory Timmons in two major wars: Vietnam and Desert Storm. He had been a soldier ever since he was old enough to enlist.

More important, he shared Timmons's views on the condition of the country.

"Immigrants," he had told his company in a private meeting a few days earlier, "are milking us for everything they can get. Asians. Mexicans. Africans. Even the Russians are flooding through the ports of entry to take advantage of our generosity.

"And what do we get in return? Crime. Gangs. Drugs."

One by one, his men nodded. The Phantom Company, as they were known, was made up of career Green Berets and mercenaries who shared Blake's views.

"What does this current administration do about the situation? To pay for these new leeches, they tax decent Americans far beyond their means to pay. And when these ordinary citizens voice their anger by refusing to pay the tax blackmail, the administration sends in troops of federal agents to kill them."

Indoctrination sessions were held monthly to make sure the troops kept the goals of the company in focus.

Timmons had called him several hours earlier to ask for ten men to deliver crates to a farm in Alabama.

Blake asked no questions and stated that the men would be ready in an hour.

THE DELIVERY WAS MADE. The soldiers helped Scott and his people hide the cache of weapons behind a false wall in the barn behind the main house.

Several other men had shown up at the farm, and Blake recognized their leader from his tour of duty in Vietnam. A French Algerian. He didn't know the man's name, but it didn't matter. Every time they met, he had a different one.

"Good to see you, *mon ami,*" the man said, shaking the captain's hand.

"What are you doing here?"

"The colonel thought you could use a hand."

While the fatigue-clad soldiers hauled crates into the barn, the Algerian took his men on a tour of the barn, then the house.

As Blake and his men drove away from the Scott farm down the dirt path that led to the county highway, he could see the Algerian and his men unloading large, heavy canvas bags and carrying them into the house.

BOLAN ORDERED COFFEE from the waitress, then got up and made a phone call. The call traveled through a series of cutouts, to eventually ring in Hal Brognola's office at Stony Man Farm. The soldier briefed him on his plans.

The big Fed asked him to hold on for a minute, then came back on the telephone.

"After your call I had some of the Stony Man Farm personnel see if they could find the sources of the leaks."

"Did they?"

"I'm not sure. One of the blacksuits at the Farm mentioned once serving with a real crackpot by the name of Captain Leslie Blake. Supposedly, he tried to convince men under his command that the country is going to hell partly because of immigration policy. Blake's been under surveillance at his office, and a look-see by one of our snoops came up with Byron Scott's name and address scribbled on a scrap of paper."

"Where is Blake's posting?"

"At an arsenal outside of Montgomery, Alabama. At one time, he served under Colonel Timmons, who, according to military records, was General Mark Lawrence's right-hand man for years."

Bolan shook his head. The lieutenant who led an attack on him came to mind. Now a Captain Blake, and a Colonel Timmons. And all served under General Mark Lawrence.

Was the military planning some kind of coup and using protest groups they secretly provided with weapons as the excuse to take over the government? He decided to hold the question until he saw Brognola in person. Security at the Farm was as tight as it could get, but no system was infallible.

REJOINING HIS TEMPORARY team at a plastic-topped table, Bolan filled them in on what Brognola had told him, and he repeated the option to the two deputies of not joining him on the mission.

"Forget it," Frank Tallchief said bluntly. "Anything we should know about the group or the weapons?"

"According to the information I got over the telephone, a number of the members of Scott's group have been hassled by overzealous IRS agents. The husband of one of them was even killed by federal cops when he started a shooting war to stop the tax men from foreclosing on his home.

"The rest are just out for blood. My informant's opinion is that it doesn't matter that it's taxes that they're protesting, or their right to brew whiskey and sell it. They're blood hungry."

WHEN THEY REACHED the dirt road that led to Byron Scott's farmhouse, the soldier pulled off the road and hid the car behind a tall stand of bushes.

Checking his wristwatch, he told his companions that they would move out at dark. While he waited for the sun to go down, the Executioner slipped out of his jacket, pants and shirt. The blacksuit he wore under them was better cover at night.

Arming himself with the silenced 9 mm Beretta, the mammoth .44 Magnum Desert Eagle and the Applegate-Fairbairn combat blade, Bolan slipped one of the pair of Uzis in the canvas bag onto a shoulder. He then filled the pockets of the combat vest he'd donned with extra magazines and clipped four incendiary grenades to hooks hanging from the garment.

Lifting the heavy dufflelike bag, he turned to the deputies.

Both men wore .357-caliber Colt Pythons in their waist holsters and gripped M-16 A-2 assault rifles.

"Got enough magazines?" Bolan asked.

"More than enough," Proudfoot replied.

The soldier turned to Tallchief.

"You might want to mount your M-203 under your Colt. You'll never know when a grenade launcher will come in handy."

The heavyset Indian nodded in agreement and dug deep under the front seat. When he returned, the M-203 was ready for firing, loaded with a 40 mm missile. Hanging from a webbed belt around his waist were four more grenades.

"Now I'm ready."

"We walk from here."

Bolan led the way up the hill, stopping to check that nobody was observing them.

All was clear.

They reached the farmhouse, and saw that a dozen vehicles were parked in the large, unpaved area at one side of the building.

Bolan crept forward and looked through the windows.

Nobody.

He scanned the immediate area, then narrowed his focus on the barn and pointed to it.

"In there," he said. "That's where they are."

The soldier led the two men through the bushes that surrounded the house and barn, stopping behind a stack of logs.

"Wait here," he whispered.

Bolan spent the next ten minutes carefully seeding the perimeter of the barn with packets of explosives, set to detonate in thirty minutes.

Bolan slipped into the building after picking the lock on a side door. The deputies had offered to join him, but this was a one-man job.

The soldier could hear the muffled sounds of talking. He moved quietly to a door, and, with Beretta in hand, he eased it open an inch and looked inside.

It was empty, but the muffled sounds were louder.

Moving into the office, he searched for another door.

A soft, creaking sound caught his attention. Quickly, he flattened against a wall. The Beretta in his hand was set on automatic fire.

A section of wall in the office began to turn inward on hidden hinges. A large man came through the opening, cradling a Striker 12 in his arms.

Bolan knew the weapon. Drug dealers called it the Street Sweeper, and he had once seen it used for "crowd control" of a brutal and bloody sort, by white policemen in South Africa.

A cross between a shotgun and a large revolver, the Striker 12 could release a dozen shotgun shells from its coffee-can-shaped magazine in a few seconds. What it lacked in accuracy, it made up in killing power.

In most hands, the weapon was impossible to control. If fired from the shoulder, the powerful recoil would overcome any but the most massively built shooters. The thugs who stuck with the gun always fired it from the hip.

Bolan waited until the armed man moved past him in the dark, then wrapped a forearm around the gunner's neck. As the guy struggled to free himself, the Executioner increased the pressure on the windpipe, until finally the man was limp. Ramming a dirty rag into the guy's mouth and cuffing his hands behind his back with plastic riot cuffs, Bolan pulled the unconscious gunner to a desk and shoved him under it.

Moving to the edge of the wall opening, the soldier studied the hidden room. Ten men and a woman sat in front of a large cache of military hardware.

Bolan peeked inside and saw the crates stacked against the walls.

According to the markings he could read from his vantage point, the crates contained assault rifles, automatic pistols, a variety of ammunition and explosives.

A coughing sound behind him made Bolan turn quickly. The unconscious man was beginning to stir. The Executioner yanked him to his feet and led him out the side door.

The Jeep was parked against the side of the barn. The two deputies lost the bored expressions on their faces when they saw Bolan.

The soldier removed the gag from his prisoner's mouth. "Start talking."

"About what?"

"Who are the people in that room and why are you all there?"

"Just...just friends," the man stuttered, terrified of the Beretta Bolan had pressed against his temple.

"That's not good enough."

"Really. That's all we are—friends getting together," the man whined.

Proudfoot stepped up to the frightened man, then turned toward his cousin.

"Rattlesnake dance," he grunted.

The Tax Resisters' Alliance member shuddered. "They're just foolin' around, aren't they?" he asked Bolan.

The soldier shrugged. "They're full-blooded Cherokees, and they've got a hundred years of resentment against the white man."

Proudfoot studied the captive. "We need four...maybe five full-grown rattlesnakes."

The frightened man looked at Bolan. "What is...this rattlesnake dance?"

"We put you in a hole with snakes," Proudfoot stated. "You dance around and try not to let snakes bite you."

"Wait," the man whined. "Byron Scott is head of it. It was his idea."

"What idea?"

"To get guns and explosives and go after IRS offices. Some of us wanted to call the IRS and warn them about the bombs,'' the terrified captive added.

Bolan stared at him cynically. ''I'll bet you did.''

He turned to Proudfoot and Tallchief. ''Keep an eye on this guy. I'll handle the rest.''

''Need a hand?'' Tallchief asked.

''I'll yell if I do.''

Bolan returned the Beretta to its holster. Then, filling his pockets with packets of plastic explosive, he made a circle of the barn, attaching a block of C-4 to the walls every one hundred feet.

Quickly, he moved around the building again to make sure the timers were set for twenty minutes, then slipped back into the building.

He had just finished attaching the last of the C-4 to the wall between the office and the arms storeroom when he heard a voice call out, ''Hey Jimmy Joe, where the hell are you?''

Bolan unleathered his Beretta as a squat man in his late thirties stepped through the opening into the office.

The soldier held the gun against the man's neck.

''Shh,'' he whispered.

''Go to hell,'' the man yelled as he twisted the

9 mm MAC-10 he was carrying into firing position.

"You first," Bolan replied, and pulled the trigger.

A pair of silenced 9 mm Parabellum rounds tore apart the stout man's throat. He staggered from the impact of the slugs and fell backward into the hidden storeroom, spewing blood onto the floor.

At the sight of the bloodied corpse, the men and woman grabbed the weapons on the floor next to their chairs.

Bolan stepped into the room, his Uzi blazing a continuous stream of burning lead.

Two would-be terrorists dropped to the floor as the slugs tore across their stomachs. A third man pulled hard on the trigger of his AK-74 assault rifle. But the impact of 9 mm rounds from the soldier's Uzi threw him off balance, so the few rounds he fired ripped holes in the wooden roof.

Bolan brought him down with a sustained burst, then grabbed at the canvas belt around his waist for a fragmentation grenade.

He jumped backward into the office and dived to the floor as the armed bomb landed in the middle of six men and detonated.

Scrambling to his feet, the soldier ejected the

spent clip and slammed a full magazine into the subgun.

Led by the sole woman, six men saturated with shrapnel from the grenade rushed into the office. Like furious wasps, they attacked in every direction, unleashing an awesome volume of lead across the length and width of the room.

Bolan had anticipated the move and had flattened himself against the wall that hid the door to the storeroom.

He waited for the ear-shattering cascade to stop, then stepped in front of the attackers and pointed the squat weapon at them.

One man spun as several rounds ripped open a cavity in his chest. A second gunner was too hasty in responding to the Executioner's assault.

Bolan had jumped out of the path as soon as he had fired, and the projectiles from the gunman's weapon dug into a concrete-block wall. He waited for the attacker to turn back to him, then put him out of his misery with a 3-round burst that shattered the man's sternum.

As best as he could count, he had twenty rounds left in the Uzi's magazine, and a lot of terrorists to still bring down.

He could see the woman egging the others on.

"Drop it, lady," he ordered.

"Screw you!" she snapped, and started to squeeze the trigger of the Tec-9 in her hands.

A look of regret flashed across Bolan's face as he drilled three rounds into the woman's chest.

Grabbing a second frag grenade from his web belt, he pitched it at the wave of men trying to fire at him, then ducked behind a metal desk and pressed his face into the floor.

He could hear screams as the frag bomb exploded, which were followed by the sounds of moaning from a handful of dying men.

Glancing over the top of the desk, he could see that the floor between him and the weapons storage room was littered with body parts of men who, less than a hour ago, were planning the deaths of innocents who happened to be in one of the IRS offices when they bombed them.

None of the terrorists were still standing.

Bolan checked his watch. Six minutes remained before the C-4 reduced the building to rubble.

Running from the wooden building, he stopped to pull the captured terrorist from the Jeep, and shoved him behind a tall stack of hay. He signaled the two deputies. "Time to get out of here," he ordered as he started the engine, then raced away as he heard the first of the explosions.

THE ALGERIAN LISTENED to the explosion from over the hill. Even in the dark, the momentary sunlight created by detonating explosives and ammo revealed bits of shattered wood spraying skyward.

Mack Bolan had found another route to the farm buildings. From what he had heard about the man, it wasn't unusual for him to face impossible odds and come out the victor.

He turned to the team he had brought.

"That noise was this man Bolan," he warned. "Everybody take cover. He should be driving down the dirt road very soon."

Then he flattened himself behind a low bush and steadied the late-model Russian-made AK-74 assault rifle against his cheekbone.

Very soon now, he would earn the large bonus Timmons had promised him for killing the American government's mercenary.

CHAPTER TWENTY-FOUR

Bolan tried to stare through the curtain of darkness. Every instinct warned him there was someone hidden and waiting to kill him. As he carefully peered into the untilled fields that surrounded him and his companions, he listened intently for sounds of an enemy.

The wooded land past the farm was alive with noises of living creatures. He could hear the sounds of the birds, of small animals scurrying along the ground, searching for food.

A profusion of trees, shrubs, wild flowers and plants competed with one another for space on the unkempt land. If Scott was ever a farmer, it had to have been many years ago. The land looked as if it hadn't felt the blade of a plow for a long time.

Billy Proudfoot lightly touched his shoulder.

"People are hiding down the hill," he whispered.

"I know. I guess I didn't get all of them."

Frank Tallchief joined them. "Who are they?"

"My best guess is mercenaries hired to take me out," the soldier replied.

"How do you want to proceed?" Proudfoot asked.

"Find out where each of them is hidden and put them out of action," the Executioner replied.

Bolan led the way down the hill, stopping near an outcropping.

"One of you shoots from here," he ordered. "And wait until you actually see somebody before you fire."

Proudfoot nodded and hid behind the large crop of rock, checking the magazine in his M-16 as he dropped into a squat.

The Executioner studied the terrain ahead of him. There was a stand of bushes on his left. Turning to Tallchief, he pointed.

"Suit you?"

"Good as any place," Tallchief replied, and slipped away to plant himself behind the thick growth of vegetation.

Soft thuds from behind a stand of pines drew Bolan's attention, and he turned to see a half-dozen fatigue-clad men running toward him, their MAC-10s spewing a steady stream of lead in his direction.

These were trained fighters that had a target they wanted to destroy.

Him.

Bolan dived behind a stand of trees, which was a poor shield. But at least the trees provided him with temporary cover until he could calculate his next move.

The soldier tried to decide who had sent the gunners. The names of Blake, Timmons and Lawrence came to mind. Who told them where he would be—and when? Only Hal Brognola knew.

And Brognola couldn't be the source.

Like a wraith, the Executioner streaked toward the startled mercenaries, arming and pitching a frag grenade, then switched to a two-handed grip on the Uzi. As the bomb ripped the center flank of the enemy, shrill cries of agony shattered the stillness of the night. The handful of shadows started to vanish deeper into the dark.

Someone hollered an order. "Stand and fight, or die!"

The gunmen stopped and turned back.

Bolan noted that the survivors all wore Army fatigues and gripped either MAC-10s or M-16s.

A gunner suddenly charged in a burst of bravado, accompanied by loud, incoherent shouting.

The Executioner set his Uzi on automatic, tracked the movement of the lead attacker and fired. The rounds caught the man in the upper chest and whirled him to the ground.

The surviving force rushed him, spraying 5.56 mm on the run. Calmly Bolan snapped a fresh 30-round magazine into his weapon, and jacked the first round into the chamber.

He moved to the right and hunched down to wait until the enemy came closer. Then he jumped to his feet, gripping the Uzi in both hands.

Bolan wondered who had supplied the attackers with the latest in American weaponry, the M-16 A-2, even as he felt the burning slash of tiny slivers of shredded wood chopping a chunk of skin from his left cheek as bullets ricocheted off the trees.

He didn't waste time sighting the Uzi. He fired the powerhouse rounds in the magazine from the hip, turning the enemy gunners into lifeless bags of bleeding skin and shattered bones in less than five seconds.

His senses told him there were no enemies left alive in the area.

"Frank. Billy," he called in a loud whisper.

"Over here," a voice replied.

Moving cautiously through the brush, the soldier saw Proudfoot on his knees.

"Are you all right?"

Proudfoot nodded. "Frank isn't."

Frank Tallchief was resting on his cousin's lap, his eyes glazed with the finality of death.

A good partner, a fine human being, had been sacrificed to stop a band of murderers from killing innocent people.

There was nothing either one of them could do for the dead deputy.

"I'll help you carry his body to the Jeep," Bolan offered.

Proudfoot rejected the offer.

"I can do it," he said, lifting the body to the vehicle and gently placing it on the rear seat.

Bolan got in the Jeep and started the engine. As he drove away, he wondered if those they had killed were worth the life of somebody like Frank Tallchief.

He didn't think so.

Proudfoot would bury his cousin, and Bolan would exact revenge.

CHAPTER TWENTY-FIVE

Sheriff Doug Handler had driven Bolan to the airport in Asheville. A short time later, the soldier got off the plane at Washington National Airport. As usual, he studied everything and everyone.

Stopping at the Hertz rental agency, he arranged for a midsize car, then waited for the security attendant to bring his special canvas bag from the cockpit.

Bolan showed the airport-security representative the federal identification card Brognola had provided him. Then, exchanging the bag for a ten-dollar tip, he walked outside to where the rental cars were parked.

A black Cadillac Brougham waited at the curb. Inside were two hard-faced men looking uncomfortable in their business suits. They didn't even seem to notice him.

Probably plainclothes bodyguards waiting for

some big shot, Bolan decided as he let his gaze run down the rows of parked cars in the main lot. Here and there, cars were pulling in or out. No one in them seemed to be looking at him.

The Hertz bus drove him to where the rental car was parked. Again he checked to make sure he wasn't being watched.

So much for being careful, he told himself as he got in the car and started it.

Pausing to slip on the shoulder holster that carried his silenced 9 mm Beretta 93-R, and the rigid leather case in which he wore his massive .44-caliber Desert Eagle, he checked that both weapons were loaded and cocked, then slipped them into their holsters, and drove out of the parking enclosure.

The top of the canvas carryall that contained the rest of his traveling armory was unzipped and sat on the seat next to him, ready to provide him with a variety of kill tools, ranging from a 9 mm Uzi to 40 mm fragmentation grenades.

Bolan entered the George Washington Memorial Parkway, which paralleled the slow-moving Potomac River. Still wary, the soldier checked the traffic behind him in the rearview mirror.

It was one of the rare times when he'd lucked out. There were almost no cars on the road, just a black Cadillac Brougham that had entered the parkway behind him.

The soldier noted the possibility that it could be the same one that had been parked at the main terminal curb, then shifted his thoughts to other matters at hand.

Brognola had contacted him via Handler about new information, and the Executioner was on the way to a meet with the big Fed to review the results of his mission.

Idly, he looked at the Potomac River that edged the parkway. It was a clear autumn day, unusually warm for September. Private boats filled the water, as owners took advantage of the mild weather.

Bolan glanced at the clock mounted in the dashboard. It wasn't yet six in the morning, so traffic was almost nonexistent. Bureaucrats didn't seem to believe in beating the sun out of bed just to get to work.

He looked in the rearview mirror. The boat-long Cadillac was still behind them, and he wondered when it was going to exit the parkway.

Wariness returned, and he decided to slow and see if it passed him. The vehicle maintained its position behind him.

Glancing back, he saw the two expressionless

men in the front seats of the car. There was no one in the back seat. So, no pickup at the airport.

Bolan eased the Desert Eagle out of his belt holster and tucked it between his thighs.

Traffic was fortunately sparse. It was time to find out what these guys were about.

The Executioner pushed down hard on the accelerator. The midsize rental car tore ahead in response to the surge of gasoline-generated energy.

Glancing in the side-view mirror, he saw the large dark vehicle moving quickly to catch up to him.

He was the target. No doubt.

A look in his rearview mirror revealed a flash of reflected sunlight as the passenger held a Tec-9 out his window.

Over the rush of wind slamming against his car, Bolan could hear the soft thuds of slugs glancing off his vehicle. The chunks of hot lead cut grooves in the skin of his car as he kept trying to present as small a profile as he could to them.

The soldier decided to try another tactic.

He jammed on the brakes. The Cadillac almost slammed into his rear, then swerved and moved up to parallel his window.

Steering with his right hand, Bolan grabbed the big .44 pistol in his left hand and shoved it out of his window, aiming at the other vehicle. As he fired several rounds, he saw the wide-faced man framed in the opened window drop his gun and grab for his face, then saw his lips part as he screamed in agony.

The soldier couldn't risk an accident by taking his eyes off the road. Guessing at the direction, he rapidly pumped two more rounds at the sound of the screaming man.

He heard the plinking sound of brass cases bouncing against his door, and the high-pitched whine as one of the hot lead slugs ricocheted from the edge of the window.

Bolan risked a glance at the other car and saw the man slide out of view.

The driver raised a squat, ugly automatic pistol in his right hand and started to fire wildly at him. Bolan tried to return the fire, then heard the ominous metallic click as the Eagle's hammer hit metal.

There was no time to drop the clip and snap in a new one. All he could do was try to outrun the other car.

He dragged the canvas bag closer, thrust a hand inside and grabbed the Uzi. He knew it was cocked.

Turning his head quickly, he peppered the right

side of the Cadillac's windshield with 9 mm rounds.

Several ricocheted off the mounted rearview mirror and found their way into the interior of the large car. Through the mirror mounted above his windshield he saw the driver vanish from sight.

Like an enraged elephant, the driverless Cadillac went berserk, twisting its way in a figure-eight pattern across the road, narrowly missing a station wagon coming in the opposite direction.

As Bolan watched, the metallic behemoth crashed at full speed into a wire barrier on the edge of the road and stopped momentarily. Suddenly, the gas tank ruptured and exploded into a brilliant ball of flame.

A body flew through the metal framework that had once held a front windshield and rolled across the highway, stopping a few feet from the rental car.

Bolan shoved open his door, got out and hurried to the corpse. He nudged the body on the ground with a toe, aiming his submachine gun at the gunner's head in case the gunman was just pretending.

Satisfied the enemy was dead, he knelt and turned him over. What remained of the face was covered with blood-soaked dirt. Much of the neck had been shot away. He looked at the overturned car and saw the other body trapped inside the twisted metal.

Bolan searched the pockets of the dead pair.

Nothing.

Then he saw the plain metal necklaces around their necks. Dog tags. He yanked them off and dropped them into a jacket pocket. He'd have Brognola check them out later.

But he suspected the gunners had been sent by somebody who had been tipped off that he was returning to Washington and when he was arriving.

The sound of police and fire sirens got louder. Bolan didn't have the luxury of time to explain his presence, or who he thought the dead men were.

He drove away in the rental car before the police arrived and detained him for questioning.

CHAPTER TWENTY-SIX

The meeting between Colonel Timmons and General Lawrence was brief. Lawrence was livid.

"Ten professionals. All dead," he exploded. "Plus the same number of members of the protest group. Who the hell is this Bolan, the devil?"

"All we can do is keep trying to get him," Timmons replied.

"You've got to do better than that. I want him dead!"

The phone rang. Reluctantly, Lawrence answered it.

"Hold him for a moment," the general said to his secretary on the other end of the line.

"McCutcheon calling me. He must have gotten news of what happened in Lynchville."

Timmons left the room.

Lawrence spoke into the telephone. "Put him on."

There was a short pause while the general listened.

"I just heard about it. We're working on alternate plans."

Another pause for listening ensued.

"I don't know if Alan Macomb knew about the plans to attack the tax protest group."

Still another pause.

"The President is sending him to your birthday party? I wasn't planning to show up. But I just changed my mind. Maybe between the two of us—and some of my men—we can find out what's going on."

IF ALAN MACOMB HADN'T come, the birthday party would have been a smashing success. However, one couldn't refuse a request from the President of the United States to have his chief of staff represent him at the birthday party.

McCutcheon supposed that in such a large group one could ignore the presence of Macomb. Still, the former senator's reputation for demanding that Congress enact laws that make the actions of the more violent protest groups a crime protest wouldn't sit well with McCutcheon's constituents if they read in one of the gossip columns that he had been seen in the home of someone as dedi-

cated to freedom of speech and the right to bear
arms as Harvey McCutcheon.

The President couldn't have picked a worse
time to force Macomb's presence on him. The tall
gray-haired man painted a smile on his face and
continued to wander around the room, stopping to
chat for a moment with each cluster of guests.

It was the usual group, the rest of the senators
who looked to him for leadership on antiarma-
ment legislation, the newly minted millionaires,
some of the Embassy Row crowd, anxious to stay
on his good side. The pair of armed bodyguards
who worked for him stared suspiciously at everybody, including each other.

McCutcheon stared at the chief of staff, wondering why the former senator had decided to
come. It wasn't because they were old friends.
They had been rivals from their first days in
Washington as young congressmen.

The two of them had agreed on nothing over
the years. Macomb was the kind of liberal who
would defend the rights of Commies to speak out
in public about their beliefs. He'd backed the in-
famous Selma, Alabama, march to support racial
equality, as well as the integration of schools.

So far, it had been a very successful year. For
the most part, the protest groups were satisfied.

Lawrence had done a good job keeping them provided with weapons and ammunition.

A few of the groups, the senator had to admit, were even too racist for him. But all of them made donations to his personal campaign fund. What they didn't know was that no such fund actually existed.

The money was sent monthly to a private bank in the Grenadine Islands, where it continued to earn interest for him.

Yes, he decided, a very successful year. Even if he didn't get nominated by his party, McCutcheon knew he had banked more than enough money to live like a king anyplace he wanted.

And soon to be even more successful, he reminded himself as he observed the tall military man enter the room: General Mark Lawrence, hero, handsome and smart. Everything somebody need to go into politics.

McCutcheon gestured to the butler, who came over. "Have the musicians start playing. I'll cut the cake in a half hour."

The butler nodded, then walked to where five musicians sat chatting and signaled them.

The music began. As the senator watched, couples drifted to the sides of the room. Several reappeared in the center, this time dancing.

He glanced to where the general had been talking to reporters. It was almost a requirement that parties thrown in the Washington area include a few columnists and television people.

An attractive blond woman kept throwing questions at Lawrence. McCutcheon knew her—Wendy Waterman, who cohosted a morning news show. She had a reputation for getting hidden information even when the best of her competitors had failed.

McCutcheon signaled the general to follow him.

Lawrence walked into the richly furnished study and waited for the senator to enter before he shut and locked the door.

"That woman reporter. Be careful of her. She eats heroes for breakfast," McCutcheon warned.

"We just chatted about how I had happened to know you."

"That's what I mean. She'll twist your words and make us sound like we're coconspirators in some devious plot."

Lawrence smiled coldly. "In a way we are."

The senator changed the subject. "How much did Timmons collect this month?"

Lawrence looked furious. "Nothing."

McCutcheon looked stunned, then suspicious.

"Where did the money go?"

"There was no money. Instead, two of our more powerful supporters have been killed. Potter, of the Carolina Militia as you know, and the majority of his men, as well as Lodge and his WAR bikers."

"Bolan?"

Lawrence's voice was filled with rage. "Yes, Bolan, a murderous maniac who thinks he knows what's good for the country. He's a psychopathic killing machine."

"What was in it for him to kill them?"

"The President asked for his help," the general replied coldly.

"I wish I could play the tape that my contact made of that ass in the White House giving the order to this Bolan. I could nail him to the cross on the floor of the Senate."

Lawrence wouldn't identify Lillian Henshaw. Not as long as she was useful to him.

The senator stopped his pacing and stared at Lawrence.

"Your contact actually heard him tell this Bolan to go out and kill Potter, Lodge and their people?"

"Not in so many words," Lawrence admitted. "But it doesn't take a Rhodes Scholar to figure out what the President wanted the hired merc to do.''

Thinking about Lawrence's words, the senator decided to wait before making them public.

''If you went before the press and told them what the President said, I'm not sure too many people would believe you. Especially if Macomb calls you a liar.

''And I've known that man for more than twenty years. He would call you a liar, if it suited his personal agenda at the time.''

The general looked frustrated. ''Any ideas?'' he asked.

Senator McCutcheon nodded. ''If Alan Macomb died in an accident, there would be nobody to dispute your statements. I think we could even call for impeachment proceedings. Now all you have to do is figure out the kind of accident that kills the chief of staff,'' McCutcheon said with a smile.

He was confident the general would.

''What about Bolan—is there any chance he'll show up here?''

''I wouldn't be surprised.''

''But that means he knows all about our...arrangement,'' McCutcheon gasped. ''The house is full of very important people.''

He stared at the general. "How do you know he's coming?"

Lawrence thought of Lillian Henshaw and their lovemaking the previous night. In the morning, she had told him to be careful since Alan Macomb had been asked by the President to stand in for him at McCutcheon's birthday party.

McCutcheon continued to voice his concern. "What if he comes here? There are reporters all over the place."

"He won't. I've got ten of my best fighters waiting for him to show his face."

"I hope you also have an explanation for the shooting."

"We just found out Bolan was a Soviet spy." He paused. "They still have them, you know, despite all the bullshit about peaceful coexistence."

ALAN MACOMB STEPPED onto the patio to light a long cigar. Looking around to make sure he was alone, he walked to the set of steps at the end of the flagstone veranda and watched as part of the shadows of trees and bushes separated from the others.

"Hal told me you'd be here," the White House chief of staff said softly to the moving shadow.

Bolan was fully garbed for battle, his weapons loaded and ready for combat.

"Is General Lawrence here?" he asked.

Macomb nodded. "He just arrived. McCutcheon and he went into a small room." Then he added, "He didn't come alone."

He looked at the street.

"There are four cars parked along the curb. They followed the general from the Pentagon to here. I'd guess there are more than a dozen Special Forces types armed to the teeth waiting in them for a signal from Lawrence."

He started toward the soldier.

"Look straight ahead, as if you were alone," the Executioner snapped in a low voice. "That will just make it a little more difficult."

The chief of staff turned his head away and stared out into the streets of the small Virginia town where McCutcheon lived.

He repeated the question. "To do what?"

"Kill."

"Who?"

"Maybe me, if I showed up. Maybe you." Then he asked, "What do you know about Lawrence and McCutcheon?"

"I served with Harvey in the Senate. He's what I call a rogue politician. The best that money can buy. This new act of his—defending the rights of groups to bear arms, to riot and to kill people—is his way of getting reelected before anybody checks into any offshore bank accounts he has.

"All I really know about Lawrence is that he's a widower. His wife and daughter were caught in the middle of a gang shootout in San Francisco. He was some kind of hero in Vietnam. At least he won a lot of medals, and a lot of men look up to him as if he were the second coming of Christ. My memory says he was a black-and-white sort of commanding officer. His way was right. Every other way was wrong."

Macomb pretended to study the stars in the sky. "Rumors have it that the other national party is thinking about putting him up as a candidate for the presidency. They think he can win by appealing to the racist gangs, the antigovernment groups and frightened nuts just like them."

"He just might. There are a lot of people fed up with excessive government control. And even more who wondered why we ever let nonwhites enter the country."

Macomb interrupted him. There was no fear in his voice as he asked, "Should I stick around or leave?"

"One more question before I answer," Bolan

said. "Any word on who's been leaking the information about me?"

"The President's secretary put together a list of everyone who works in the White House. As I'm sure you know, the Man has asked Milt Andrews, head of the White House Secret Service detail, to head up the investigation."

The President's aide sneaked a glance at the Executioner's face. Bolan looked satisfied.

"I have a short message for you from the President." Macomb hesitated until he sensed Bolan's interest. "He said to tell you we don't need to make either Lawrence or McCutcheon a martyr. There has to be another way."

Before the soldier could respond, the chief of staff turned to go back inside, then stopped and turned back. He reached inside his jacket pocket.

"Hal didn't say so, but I think he agrees with my boss. He asked me to give you this if I happened to run into you. Just so you know it really came from him, he said to use the word Striker. What the hell is Striker?"

"Another time," Bolan said. "About your leaving. It might not be a bad idea. All hell is going to break loose in a little while, and bullets have a habit of ricocheting."

Macomb nodded and dropped his cigar into an

outdoor ashtray. Then he turned and walked back in the large room to retrieve his topcoat.

Bolan opened the envelope. The head of Stony Man Farm had given him information about another racist group. This one was named after a West Coast radical group that had robbed and killed to finance their white-supremacy goals. It was called The Order.

There was a suggestion at the end of the memo for Bolan to get hold of a racist piece of fiction called *The Turner Papers,* which outlined how hate groups operated to rid the United States of nonwhites.

A penciled comment at the bottom of the second page read: "A lot of scared rats are racing back into their sewers because of you. Congratulations."

Bolan smiled slightly, but he knew the war had only just begun.

The action would be brought right to the doorsteps of those he believed were feeding the hate groups weapons and lofty promises.

He waited until the chief of staff had emerged again, this time through the front door. He signaled his driver and got into the limousine.

As Macomb drove away, Bolan watched to see

if any of the four cars followed the chief of staff. None left the curb.

Now he knew. He was the target.

It was time to get ready. This time, the target would fight back. Hard.

There was no place for the enemy to hide.

CHAPTER TWENTY-SEVEN

Bolan worked his way through the shadows cast by the large number of trees surrounding the senator's estate until he came close to where the four cars were parked.

He kept his distance from the vehicles. Instead, he took out a pair of small binoculars from under his combat vest and studied the passengers.

Ten men occupied the quartet of cars. Each wore fatigues, and Bolan knew that each was fully armed and trained to kill.

Bolan didn't know if they were Special Forces, or Delta Force, or hired mercs. It didn't matter. Instinctively, he knew they were outside McCutcheon's mansion to eliminate a problem.

Him.

There was no way he could get close enough to the cars to plant plastic explosives. He would have to find another way to take them out.

He looked down at the grenades clipped to his vest.

They should get their attention.

Unclipping a frag grenade, he pulled the pin and spiraled the bomb like a football over the tops of the cars and into the street.

The explosion stunned the occupants of the vehicles. They jumped from their cars, M-16s ready to fire, and took combat positions, facing where the missile had exploded.

The soldier pitched a second missile to the right of where the first had made contact with the roadway. Startled by the second explosion, the platoon of armed gunmen rushed to the site of the second explosion. Then, looking puzzled, they turned and studied the immediate area for the location of the enemy.

Bolan pitched a third grenade into their midst.

As he flattened himself against the asphalt of the road, his ears reverberated with the deep explosive roar. Shards of shredded metal tore past him. He could feel two dig into his neck, not deep enough to do serious injury, but deep enough to hurt.

Four men had absorbed the brunt of the explosion and lay dead on the ground.

The other six ignored the bodies and fanned out, searching for the hidden assailant.

"Here," the Executioner shouted, and waited until a pair of the military hit men got closer before he washed their bodies with 9 mm lead.

The two spun from the impact and fell against two men behind them. Shoving the dead to one side, the second pair held their M-16s at their sides, squeezing the triggers.

The soldier rolled to their right, so their high-powered lead slashed through empty air. He saturated the two men with the remainder of the clip in his Uzi. Both fell to the ground in a heap.

Crouching, the Executioner hosed the final pair with a short burst, punching them to the ground.

Bolan smelled gasoline. A rapid stream of the liquid rushed into the street from a ruptured tank. A stray bullet had to have punctured the gasoline tank.

Standing back from the wreck, he emptied the rounds in the mammoth handgun at the stream of fuel, then, when it began to burn, sprinted across the road and crouched behind a parked limousine.

The relative quiet of the suburban Virginia neighborhood was suddenly shattered with the violent sound of the exploding automobile gas tank, generating a holocaust of sound compared to the grenades. Bits of torn metal flew in every direction, shattering windows and embedding themselves into the bodies of parked cars and into the walls of the stately homes that stood on both sides of McCutcheon's mansion.

The ricochet of fragments traveled like billiard balls from object to object. A huge chunk of metal crashed into the windshield of the limousine Bolan used as a shield, shattering it and spraying him with glass slivers. Another large fragment sheared through the front of the chauffeur-driven vehicle, embedding itself into the radiator.

Flames shot up from the pools of gasoline on the roadway, consuming cars and the bodies of the dead assailants in its fiery embrace.

Handsomely attired men and women had rushed out of the front door of the mansion at the sound of the exploding grenades. Now they stared in horror at the sight of burning bodies.

Bolan could see McCutcheon and the general push past the other guests and stare, expressionless, at the holocaust that had visited the neighborhood.

The general stared coldly, then promptly turned his back on the street and walked back into the house.

To call for backup, Bolan suspected.

It was time to leave. Especially since he could hear the sirens of fire engines and police cars.

There was a message he had wanted to deliver to the two men. Now he had.

Nobody was above justice. There was no place to hide.

SOUNDING THEIR ear-blasting horns, four fire trucks and five police cars converged on the area of devastation. Within minutes, ambulances arrived along with four vans from the county coroner's office, as well as several vans from local television stations.

As he donned his outerwear, Bolan was curious to hear how the senator explained the violent explosions to the press.

"This is what has happened to the security of the nation under the current administration. Gangs of criminals are permitted to roam the streets, killing innocent people at will," McCutcheon shouted into the microphones held up to him by the television reporters.

"Senator," an attractive blond woman said, "how do you explain the police finding military dog tags around the necks of the dead men they've already examined? And are the dead men currently in the military?"

McCutcheon looked to General Lawrence for help.

"I can assure all of you that there will be a full investigation by the military," the general said loudly.

Then he turned to the senator. "I think it's time we went inside and tried to comfort your guests, Senator."

The two men turned away and quickly disappeared into the mansion.

Bolan had stowed his weapons in the canvas carryall that sat on the floor of the Jeep. He got into the vehicle and started the engine. When he looked up, he saw the blond reporter standing next to the Jeep.

"Did you see what happened?" she asked.

"I stopped when I heard the explosions," he replied. "I just happened to be driving through the area."

The blonde handed him a business card.

"I'm Wendy Waterman, a reporter. If you remember seeing anything or anyone, I'd appreciate a call. Can I have your name?"

"Mike Belasko," Bolan replied.

Waterman examined him. "This doesn't look like your kind of neighborhood, Mr. Belasko."

He glanced at the mansion. "It isn't. I don't usually drive by places that smell like bullshit."

"I don't know who you are, Mr. Belasko, but you come right to the point."

"Maybe it's because I can't stand the odor of most politicians, in or out of office," the Executioner commented, then drove away before the reporter could continue the conversation.

LILLIAN HENSHAW WAS working late. The small radio on her desk was tuned to a local news station, and she gasped when she heard the news about an attempted attack on Senator McCutcheon's home. She relaxed when she heard that only the would-be assault team had been killed.

Mark Lawrence was safe. That's all that mattered.

She had been concerned when he made the decision to go into politics. The two of them could have a good life together, with his staying at the Pentagon.

As secretary to the President, she had met a lot of politicians and disliked all of them.

She hoped Mark wouldn't become like them.

Henshaw looked at the clock above her desk. It was time to leave. From the recorder that fed into the main taping system in the Oval Office, she removed an audiotape and dropped it into her purse.

As she left the office and started down the corridor toward the elevators, Milt Andrews stopped her.

"Got a minute, Lillian?"

Andrews looked like a weary bureaucrat just waiting to retire. Overweight, dressed in a wrinkled suit, his hair gray and balding on top, the older man looked more suited to handle a job shuffling papers than protecting the life of the President.

Henshaw knew he was more than that. The head of the White House Secret Service detail was one of the sharpest men she'd ever met. She didn't let his lackadaisical pose fool her.

"Sure. How can I help you?"

"I'm a little concerned about our security."

The tall, handsome brunette smiled. "I can't imagine an enemy getting past you or your men."

"Every so often, one of them does."

The President's secretary knew of the incidents. The pilot who landed his small plane on the White House lawn. The berserk man who emptied an automatic weapon at the front of the historic structure before federal police pulled him to the ground.

"You record all the President's discussions in the Oval Office, don't you?" Andrews asked.

"Only when ordered to do so by the President," she replied primly.

"What happens to those tapes?"

"They get stored in a vault so any one of them can be retrieved if the President asks for them."

"So no one gets to listen to them, except the President, afterward."

"And me, if he wants me to stay and take notes."

"You don't make extra copies of some of those tapes, do you, Lillian?" Without waiting for her reply, Andrews turned and walked away.

Inside, the woman panicked. Did they know about the tapes she'd been feeding the general? And what were they planning to do about it, if they did know?

She had to find Mark and tell him.

Their lives, and his future, might depend on it.

CHAPTER TWENTY-EIGHT

Rejecting Brognola's invitation to stay at Stony Man Farm, Bolan had found a small motel in Alexandria, Virginia, on the edge of Washington, D.C., and checked in under an alias.

His suspicion that somehow General Mark Lawrence was involved in some sort of scheme wouldn't leave him. But how did the high-ranking officer know where and when the Executioner would be so soon after he called the head of Stony Man Farm to keep him posted on his progress?

Bolan wondered briefly if Hal Brognola had changed sides. Or had the President or his chief of staff.

Nobody was above suspicion. Not when his life was on the line. He could think of nobody else who would have access to his reports.

From what Brognola had told him, the information flow went from him to the President and the chief of staff. And, supposedly, stopped there.

Not even the President's personal secretary— what was her name?—knew the contents of the verbal reports. Not unless she had somehow planted an eavesdropping device in the Oval Office.

It was a question he'd ask the Stony Man Farm chief.

"THE OVAL OFFICE, like all of the rooms in the White House, gets checked daily for listening devices," Brognola assured him when he returned his call from the small motel. "Why?"

"If you're not telling anyone outside of the committee, and the President and chief of staff aren't, why is someone always waiting in ambush when I get to where I'm going?"

"I can't answer that. The Man has Milt Andrews looking into the problem right now."

Bolan knew the head of the White House detail of the Secret Service. Andrews was a tough, honest cop with the tenacity of a bulldog. The soldier knew that the gray-haired man wouldn't stop looking until he found the answer.

The problem was, Bolan couldn't wait. He had knocked down a lot of hornets' nests, and armed hornets were beating the bushes, trying to find him.

Bolan reached for the envelope that Macomb had passed to him at the senator's party. According to the enclosed information, The Order was after national attention. The cell that was leading the planned action was located in Maryland.

The leader of the cell was Parson Dann, the son of a former congressman. A high-school dropout, the slim young man had spent the past four years in and out of jail for assaulting nonwhite men, women and children.

Bolan noted several features about the Maryland-based group. First, they shaved their heads bald. Second, they were stealing weapons from gun shops in their area. Their preference was Uzi or MP-5 subguns.

An FBI undercover agent inside the gang reported that the group was planning to attack a large delegation of black diplomats from several African nations. The delegates were scheduled to meet with the President for a discussion on aid to their countries.

All the head of the Bureau knew was when the delegation was coming, and that they had made arrangements for a special train to bring them to Washington, D.C., from New York, after the leaders of the group spoke at a Madison Square Garden rally.

"How far do you want me to go with this Dann character, since his father was a famous congressman?"

"As far as you have to," Brognola replied.

"What do you know about the President's secretary?" Bolan asked.

The big Fed was surprised at the question. "Why?"

"She was the only outsider who could have eavesdropped on your meetings."

The head of Stony Man Farm reflected about what he really knew about her.

"Lillian Henshaw was a secretary in the Pentagon. Handled top-security work."

"Who'd she work for?"

"Here's a name that's cropped up before—General Mark Lawrence."

"Is she married?"

"I don't think so."

"Does she ever get together with Lawrence?"

"If she does, it's on the sly. But let me do some deeper digging and I'll call you back."

LILLIAN HENSHAW MANAGED to get out of the White House for an hour.

"There's something I have to exchange at Woodward & Lathrop Department Store," she told one of the other secretaries.

Making sure nobody was following her, the woman slipped into a phone booth and called the general on his private line.

"Sorry, but the general is in a meeting with the secretary. Can I take a message?"

"Who is this?"

"Sergeant Carter."

Henshaw knew Carter was one of the general's closest aides.

"I'm going to play a tape for you. Copy the information and give it to the general."

Carter scribbled notes on a pad of white paper as he listened.

When the tape was over, the White House secretary asked, "Did you get it?"

"Yes. Bolan should be arriving at the skinheads' clubhouse by eleven."

She hung up the phone, checked again to see if anyone was watching her and, dropping the tape and the miniature tape player back into her purse, she walked to the nearest exit and hailed a cab.

WENDY WATERMAN WAS surprised by the call. She hadn't really expected Mike Belasko to ever call her.

"Nice surprise," she said. "Business or social?"

"Business."

"Shame." She sighed. "How can I help you?"

"Check your files for any information on two people. Parson Dann and Lillian Henshaw."

As Bolan held, she typed in the name "Parson Dann."

A record of criminal activities appeared on the screen. She read them to the man on the other end of the line.

"What about the woman?"

She repeated the process for Lillian Henshaw, and a much shorter list appeared. She read the report into the telephone.

"Lillian Henshaw. Age thirty-nine. Born Costa Mesa, California. Served in the military as a commissioned officer. Highest rank achieved was captain. For the past two years has been the President's personal secretary."

"Any information on whom she served under?"

Waterman switched to another screen.

"She was an aide to General Mark Lawrence until she resigned to join the White House staff."

There was silence on the other end of the line, then Bolan asked another question. "Could you check your records about what functions General Lawrence runs?"

She cleared the computer screen and typed in the military man's name.

"That's strange. Between our own files and the files of other media outlets we subscribe to, we usually have more information than this."

"Than what?"

"All it says is that all requests for information regarding his current assignment should be referred to the chief Army press officer."

She kept typing, trying to get around the lack of information showing on her screen. Finally, something appeared on the computer screen.

"Did you ever hear of Phantom Company?"

She heard only silence, then the click of a telephone being placed back on its cradle.

Belasko—if that was his name—had reacted to the word "Phantom." Whom was he going to talk to about it, Lillian Henshaw or General Mark Lawrence?

Grabbing several pencils and a spiral-bound pad, Waterman slipped on her jacket and ran for the exit door.

BOLAN WAS SURPRISED. Without saying a word, he hung up the phone and leaned back on the bed in his motel room.

He hadn't heard the word for years.

Phantom was a joint Army-CIA operation to cleanse countries of terrorists, political dissidents and criminals. The secret program had been launched by a prior administration during the Vietnam conflict to eradicate insurgents. Although the military and the Central Intelligence Agency denied such an operation ever existed, it was allowed to continue on a limited scale in the United States. Its main focus was the rapid growth of antigovernment and racist groups.

From what Bolan had learned from the experts at Stony Man Farm, the field operations were carried out by mercenaries, who had no traceable affiliation with the Army or the CIA. Only in emergency situations were elements of the Army to get personally involved.

Somebody—Bolan thought he knew who—had subverted the confidential records and was trying to form the more violent of the groups into an underground movement that could destroy any efforts of the administration to put them out of business.

LAWRENCE LOOKED UP from his notes at the knock on his door.

"Enter," he called out.

The short, paunchy sergeant who took phone messages for him walked into the office.

"This just came in, sir," the noncom said, saluting.

Lawrence studied the notes. "Ask Colonel Timmons to step in here."

"Yes, sir."

The sergeant started to leave, then stopped.

"There's one more thing. As you know, we have a tap on all of the media computers in the area. Somebody inquired about Miss Henshaw's background."

The general pondered the information.

"Anything else?"

"A moment later, there was an inquiry about you."

"From the same computer?"

"Yes, sir. A local television station. Somehow they were also able to access the Phantom file.

The news disturbed Lawrence. Whoever was responsible for the trace was getting too close. It was time to sever the connecting lines.

"Did it mention any relationship between Miss Henshaw and me?"

He knew he had been very discreet in his visits to her apartment.

"Only that she was an aide to you before she moved over to the White House."

Timmons peeked into the office. Lawrence looked up and saw him.

"Good. I was just sending the sergeant to get you." He signaled the noncom to leave. Timmons shut the door.

"The sergeant told me about the skinhead information. I've already dispatched a squad to deal with Bolan."

"Good. But there's something even more important," Lawrence said. "Lillian Henshaw. How strong do you think she is?"

The colonel looked confused. "Strong? In what way?"

"If she was put under intense interrogation, do you think she would confess to providing us with notes from the committee the President has formed?"

Timmons weighed that carefully.

"She might. The only reason she has any loyalty to our efforts is her feelings about you, sir."

Lawrence nodded. "And, being a woman, her feelings can change without warning."

The colonel got the message. "Consider her handled, General."

A BODY LAY on the concrete walk that led to the front entrance of the old-fashioned apartment building. Bolan stopped the Jeep and unleathered the 9 mm Beretta, then threw his door open and got out.

He peered in both directions before he approached the body. The street was empty.

Gang shooting? There had been a surge of warfare between rival gangs in the nation's capital.

He knelt beside the woman, who was facedown. Gently, he turned her over and was shocked to see Lillian Henshaw, the President's personal secretary. Someone had pumped four rounds of lead into her chest. She was still breathing.

He started to rise so he could find a phone to call an ambulance, then realized that she wouldn't last until it got there.

Her eyes opened slowly, and she groaned softly. At first, her eyes were filled with fear, then they softened as she recognized Bolan.

"What happened?" he asked.

"Someone shot me," she mumbled.

"You looked frightened when you opened your eyes. Why?"

"I...I thought you were one of Mark's men."

It took Bolan a moment to make sense of the name she had used.

"General Mark Lawrence?"

"He's a fine man. They're using him."

She forced her hand over Bolan's.

"Don't blame him. He'd be so good for..."

Lillian Henshaw's head fell back. Bolan lowered the body to the ground. Sadly, he knew he had to leave her lying there on the sidewalk. The police would receive a call from him as soon as he found a pay phone.

Mark Lawrence had brought his private war to the door of the President's office.

Mack Bolan knew it was up to him to prevent the general from getting inside.

CHAPTER TWENTY-NINE

Getting out of her car, the blond television reporter saw the large, powerful-looking man rise from kneeling next to a body. He turned and saw her. For a moment, she thought he was the killer.

"Got a cellular phone?" Bolan yelled to her.

Numbly she nodded.

"Call the police and tell them the President's secretary has been shot," Bolan ordered.

Wendy Waterman moved closer, avoiding eye contact with the dead woman. This was the closest she had ever come to someone who had been murdered.

Finally, she managed to ask, "Who would want to kill the President's secretary?"

"Someone who wanted to silence her."

"Do you think she knew something?"

Bolan shrugged. "Obviously somebody did."

The scene was almost surreal to the young reporter. "And they killed her?"

"It's the best way to shut somebody up."

"About what?"

"Things you don't want to know about. Actions that could affect the country."

"I could help if I knew," Waterman offered. "If it's a big enough story, I can get it on the network."

Bolan shook his head, then asked, "Did you ever hear of something called *The Turner Papers?*"

The reporter had, but couldn't remember where. Then it all came back to her.

"It's some kind of sick story that's sold in almost every bookstore that peddles hate literature. A few years ago, I accompanied a police raid on an adult bookstore and asked about it. The sergeant I was with told me not to waste my time reading it. It would turn my stomach. But I read it anyway. And it did."

"The people who ordered this woman killed believe that *The Turner Papers* are a prophecy, not sick fiction."

"Let me go with you. This sounds like a story the American people are entitled to know."

The Executioner wanted no innocents along. One had already been killed.

"What makes you think that the people who had Lillian Henshaw killed would let you live to tell it? If they thought you knew who they were and what they're planning, you'd be the next to go."

Before she could stop him, Bolan got into the Jeep.

"Call the police and wait for them to show up." He hesitated, then added, "I'd appreciate it if you left me out of your report. It would only get me killed sooner than I'd like."

Then he took off down the deserted street in the direction of Georgetown.

Waterman stared after him, then remembered about making the call. When she was done, she studied the body. Somehow she was less afraid of it than when she first arrived.

Something protruded from under the corpse. The reporter knelt and picked it up.

An audiotape.

She wondered if this was why the White House secretary was killed. She would find out when she got back to the studio, filed the story and listened to the tape.

Then, afterward, if she played her cards right,

maybe Parson Dann could provide her with more information.

COLONEL TIMMONS KNOCKED on the general's office door, then opened it and entered.

Lawrence was studying yellowing newspaper clippings. He looked up at the new arrival.

"Did you know that the only people who revered General MacArthur were the soldiers who served under him?"

"No, I didn't, sir."

"A lot of people respected what he stood for and what he wanted for the country, but only his soldiers understood how far he was willing to go to achieve his goal," Lawrence added. Then he gestured to a chair in front of him. "Sit down, Colonel, and tell me how it went."

"No difficulty at all, sir."

"No nosy neighbors or police?"

"According to the Phantom merc, the street was deserted."

"I trust, Colonel, he made sure that Lillian's death was instantaneous. In view of our long relationship, I wouldn't have wanted her to suffer."

"It was immediate, according to the man."

The general studied his hands. "Good," he

commented, not looking up at his aide. "And I trust your man searched her thoroughly."

"As much as he could until he saw a car turning into the street. Then he vanished down an alley."

"Good. I can't afford to have anyone living who can lead Bolan or the President to me."

Timmons nodded. He understood. Having served the general for more than twenty years, he knew that Mark Lawrence was always careful not to leave anyone alive who could testify against him.

He could remember whole villages in South Vietnam that the general had destroyed and their occupants killed rather than let them reveal anything of his operations to anyone, the press or superior officers.

"Then you can understand, Colonel, why I must do this."

Timmons was puzzled at the remark. He looked at the suppressed 9 mm Beretta pistol in Lawrence's right hand.

Before he could protest, the colonel felt the first of a fusillade of lead tear into his sternum. He reached out his hands to push the weapon aside, then looked down at them. Both were covered in a sticky crimson liquid.

Lifting his head to face the general, he tried to move his lips. All he wanted to know was—why.

As if Lawrence could read his mind, the senior officer answered his unasked question.

"As I just said, Colonel, I can't have anyone who can lead this Bolan or the President to me."

Calmly, he turned and dialed the sergeant's extension.

"I'm going to need someone to clean up in here, Sergeant. Someone you trust."

Lawrence checked his wristwatch. He had a date for cocktails with that stupid fool, McCutcheon, and some of the senator's supporters. There wasn't enough time to change uniforms.

Examining himself carefully, he was pleased that none of Timmons's blood had splattered him. Getting up from his chair, he ran his fingers through his hair and left.

The time for his announcement was coming. In a few short weeks, the country—no, the world— would know that Mark Lawrence wanted to be the one who'd lead his nation from the edge of disaster to a time of prosperity and peace.

As Lawrence knew, he was in a unique position to make such a commitment since he was behind so much of the domestic turmoil during the past three years.

CHAPTER THIRTY

According to Brognola's report, Parson Dann owned an ancient house in the Patterson Creek Mountains of western Maryland. It had been the home of his ancestors since the early 1700s, and they had fought in every conflict from the Revolutionary War to the Korean War.

Parson Dann was the first of the line to refuse military service. As a conscientious objector, he tried to get out of service during the Vietnam War. He was drafted despite his objections and caused enough problems to get him placed under arrest a number of times. His father, then a congressman, got his son discharged on the grounds that Parson was psychologically unfit for combat.

After the death of his father at the hands of unknown assassins, Parson inherited the entire estate, which consisted of a large parcel of land in the Patterson Creek Mountains, and barely enough money to survive.

A social misfit, Dann attracted other misfits who liked to party with him. Over a period of time, Parson Dann came to the belief that it was his destiny to destroy the government that had dared draft him—and to kill the Jews and non-whites who polluted the country his ancestors had settled.

Calling the movement The Order, the disturbed man went on a recruiting spree and convinced a variety of ex-cons, sociopaths, psychopaths and thrill seekers to join him. To pay for the weapons they needed, and the expenses of recruiting, Dann turned to holding up armored trucks and robbing small banks.

Dann wasn't stupid. He never was present at the robberies, so the only evidence authorities could use against him was that the criminals involved in the crimes were all members of The Order.

The difficulty was that all of them were fanatically loyal to the charismatic man, or terrified of revenge by his private executioners. They preferred prison to turning state's evidence.

Over the years, The Order had become a model for other racist organizations. Each success accredited to it was duplicated by similar groups across the country. So, Brognola footnoted, it was important to put them out of business.

The hardwoods and conifers competed with soft pine for space in the densely wooded area that surrounded the Dann property.

The Executioner spotted the ancient farm building several hundred yards ahead and concentrated on what he needed to do next. The structure sat in a large clearing in the dense forest.

The house looked deserted, but Bolan wasn't fooled by appearances. Too many supposedly deserted buildings in the past had housed waiting killers.

Parking his vehicle behind a stand of hardwood trees, Bolan prepared himself for a full-scale battle, stripping to his blacksuit.

The combat vest he slipped on contained an ample supply of clips for the Uzi, the Beretta and the Desert Eagle. In addition, four M-40 fragmentation grenades hung from clips for easy access.

The canvas carryall at his feet contained his traveling arsenal. Extra ammo clips and a 5.56 mm Colt M-16 A-2, fitted with a M-203 single-shot grenade launcher, lay atop the other gear, ready to be snatched up and used. An Uzi completed the armament in the bag.

A can of combat cosmetics lay next to an assortment of M-40 and 40 mm fragmentation and incendiary grenades. He liberally applied the black salve, darkening his features. He was ready.

Staying within the shadows, Mack Bolan moved toward the farmhouse.

Before Bolan could reach the target, however, automatic fire began eating up the ground around him, whining past his ears. The random strays were coming in with sudden accuracy, and the soldier whirled to find a pair of armed killers bearing down on him. One bullet tugged at his sleeve; another traced blood and searing pain across a thigh.

He fisted the suppressed Uzi and targeted both gunners with a burning spray of lead death.

The Executioner quickly checked both fallen gunmen to make sure neither was playing possum. Satisfied they were dead, he moved closer to the wooden building.

Tiptoeing to the front door, he listened for a moment, but heard no sound to indicate the presence of another person.

Bolan shoved the creaking door open with the force of his left shoulder slamming into it. A wide man with a badly botched crew cut tumbled backward into the inside front hall, losing his balance and crashing to the floor. A second shadowy figure behind rushed at the intruder.

Two more men shoved a rear door open and rushed into the room, waving MAC-10s. The first gunner started to get to his feet.

Grasping his attacker's wrist, Bolan used the man's own momentum to send him crashing into the intruder behind him. The soldier spun in one fluid movement to fend off the frontal assault by the other two. His right foot continued lifting in a high arc. The kick connected with the leading thug's rib cage, snapping bone as the would-be killer was driven back against the door frame.

The second hood tried to jump on the Executioner's back and pull him to the floor. But Bolan let his fury concentrate on the edge of his right palm as he slashed it against his assailant's carotid artery. With only a small whoosh to signal his death, the hardman fell backward against his partner.

Pushing his dead partner from him, the bulky thug reached for a long-bladed knife he'd hidden in his waistband. Then he rushed at the soldier, screeching a curse as he held the blade in the air, ready to slash.

Bolan waited until he got closer, then stepped aside and twisted the man's knife hand. Struggling, the tough tried to twist his hand free from the Executioner's grip. As he strained, concentrating every ounce of his nearly three hundred pounds in his effort to pull away, the hood broke out in a sweat. Veins on both sides of his head popped out and threatened to burst.

Bolan let the assailant's strength do the majority of the work, just making sure the blade didn't come any closer.

Finally, the fat thug gasped for air, then began to resume the battle. The hand that held the razor-sharp blade refused to do his bidding. Inch by inch, it started pushing back to his face, guided by Bolan's hand.

With one last desperate effort, he used both hands to push the man away, then the blade sliced beneath his skin and through his ribs. Consciousness faded.

Bolan let the man slide to the ground. He changed magazines on his Uzi and started on a room-by-room search. He found no one.

It was as if Parson Dann and the majority of his followers had vanished.

But where?

His curiosity was cut short by the sounds of footsteps behind him. Moving into the shadows of the hallway, he waited for the new arrival to show himself.

Whoever it was cursed softly as he or she walked into a chair. Backing away, the shadowy figure literally bumped into Bolan.

"Stand still if you like living," the soldier growled, "and turn around."

The ghostlike form did. It was the reporter, Wendy Waterman.

Bolan was both surprised and angry. "What are you doing here?"

"Looking for a story. How about you?"

"Get out of here. Now!" the Executioner ordered.

"No." The woman's reply was hard and final.

"How did you find this place?"

"From you," she replied. "Then a little digging, and I found out that Parson Dann was a first-class psychopath."

"You could be his next victim," Bolan warned.

"Or you," she snapped back. "Who knows? Maybe he'd like to see his face on television." She showed the soldier the miniature camcorder slung over a shoulder.

"More likely he'll kill you and steal your camera."

"In my experience, people are dying to get seen on television."

"In Dann's case, I hope you're right."

He had tried to dissuade the reporter from staying. The sounds of cars and motorcycles pulling up to the front door made her departure impossible. All Bolan could do was have her take cover.

She rejected his suggestion.

He pointed to an overstuffed easy chair. "When I signal for you to take cover, dive behind that chair and plaster your face and body to the floor," he ordered.

The front door opened and a tall man, his head shaved bald, walked in, carrying a MAC-10 in his right hand.

Bolan moved back into the shadows. Before he could pull Wendy Waterman back, the leader of The Order saw her. His face filled with suspicion, he growled, "Who the hell are you?"

Before she could answer, the large entranceway filled with Dann's followers. From his hiding place, Bolan counted sixteen.

Forcing herself to sound calm, the blonde introduced herself.

"How did you find my place?"

"You are listed in the telephone book. The Dann family is quite famous."

Dann continued his interrogation. "Who sent you here?"

"I figured you might have some important things to say about what was wrong with this country."

Dann laughed, then turned to the other men crowded into the living room. "What do you think?"

One of them, a thick-necked man sporting a black goatee and wearing leathers, looked at Waterman as if she were a slab of beef in a butcher shop.

"I think she'd make a nice lay for all of us," the man said, leering.

His comments were received with a smattering of applause and comments of enthusiastic agreement.

"Now, that's no way to talk about a member of the press who's about to make us all famous."

"The hell with fame," the goateed thug growled. "I want a woman."

Calmly, Dann loosed a trio of metal-jacketed rounds into the man's chest. Blood pumped out of the ruptured vessels, staining his leather jacket and dribbling down onto the wood floor.

"Don't argue with me when I make a decision," the group's leader told the dead man.

Then, stepping over the body, he signaled Waterman to follow him.

Stunned at what she had just seen, the woman stared at Parson Dann.

"That's known as discipline. You can hold your interview in the living room. It would look better on tape than a dead body in the foreground."

He gestured to two of the men to lift the body and carry it out of the room. Then he turned to a thin, nervous young man who was carrying a large satchel.

"Goofy, bring that bag with you." Looking at the blonde, he explained, "I'll bet your viewers would be impressed to see how much money is donated to the cause."

One of the other men laughed.

"I guess you could call it that, Chief. They weren't arguing when we shoved the money in the bag."

"How could they?" another man asked. "They were pushing up daisies by then."

Nervously, Waterman glanced at the shadowed area where Bolan was hiding, then followed Dann into the next room.

CHAPTER THIRTY-ONE

Mack Bolan waited in the shadows of the hallway while he planned his next move. He overheard the two guards Dann had left to watch the front entrance.

"What do you think Parson's up to?"

The second guard shrugged. "Maybe he wants to be famous."

"That means letting the girl go."

"I don't think so. Once she finishes the interview, Parson doesn't need her. He can have anybody deliver it to her station."

The first guard grinned.

"Hey, I hope I get an early crack at her. I hate having to wait."

Bolan had heard enough. It was time to move. His only concern was how to get Wendy Waterman out of the line of fire.

Softly, he crept up behind the first guard as the

second one kept staring into the living room. With a swift movement, he reached around and slashed the razor-sharp combat knife across the guard's throat.

The second guard turned to say something and saw the blood spurting from the severed blood vessels.

He look stunned, as he began to ask, "What happened to—?"

Bolan interrupted his question with a hard jab of the blade into where the neck connected to the rest of the spinal cord. Covering the second guard's mouth to prevent him from crying out, the soldier ran the blade around the neck, severing vessels and the spinal cord. He eased the bloody body to the uncarpeted floor.

DANN WAITED for the blond reporter to adjust the lens. She lifted her head and looked at the ceiling light.

"Too bad you don't have more light. The picture will be awfully dark."

From a corner of her eye, she saw Belasko standing in the doorway, signaling for her to move to the side and get down on the floor.

At first she didn't understand. Then she looked

at the men in the room, grinning at her as if she were the main course on tonight's menu.

"I'm sure we can do something about the light," Dann said. Turning to a stout, overmuscled man near him, he ordered, "Find some more lights and bring them in here."

Waterman was on her knees, peering up at the leader of the group.

Curious, he asked, "What are you doing?"

"Checking out camera angles," she replied.

Dann looked annoyed. "Where the hell is Muster? I didn't mean for him to find a camera supply store and steal lights."

He turned to the reporter. "We'll have to do with what we've got. My men are getting impatient." He looked at his watch. "And there's a train we want to catch."

The reporter looked puzzled.

The skinhead leader grinned. "We planned a little welcome for a bunch of Africans who've come to con our government out of some money." He turned to one of the oldest of the group. "Isn't that right, Linquist?"

Giggling, the flat-faced man smiled. "They'll die laughing, Parson."

Dann turned to one of the other men, a small man with a scar across his lips that formed his mouth into a permanent smile. "You went with Linquist, Tulley. Is everything ready for the train?"

"Should pass the fixed stretch of track in two and a half hours," the scarred young man answered.

Waterman pretended to be too busy with the equipment to care about the train conversation.

She nodded and pressed the camcorder against the side of her face.

The head of the group stared at her. "You know, for a reporter you aren't very nosy. Aren't you interested in what we're doing with the train?"

"It wasn't the story I came to get," the reporter replied lamely.

"Let me tell you about it." Dann pointed to the older, flat-faced man. "Linquist here worked for Amtrak as a train engineer until they caught him working drunk and canned his ass. Since then, he's been looking for a way to get even." He grinned. "We helped him find it when we heard about these Africans coming here. They're all big shots back where they come from." He laughed. "Make them think twice before coming here, even if any of them live after tonight."

He waited for the blonde to ask questions.

Shaking under the pants outfit she wore, Waterman knew she had to ask a few questions or arouse suspicions from the group leader.

"How are you going to deal with these... visitors?"

"Terry here," Dann replied, "pulled the bolts on a section of track that crosses a deep ravine."

"Don't the railroads have signaling devices to warn them about problems on the tracks?"

The ex-railroad employee started to laugh.

"That's why we needed a train expert like Linquist. He soldered a strip of electrical wire to the section of track we played with, so the train will get a continuous signal that everything's fine ahead."

"Are the Africans the only ones on the train?" Waterman asked.

"Naw. The train left New York full. Government types spending the day in New York before going home to Washington, D.C. Probably a couple hundred people."

"Won't they be killed, as well?"

"Serves them right for being on the same train as those Africans."

He turned away from the reporter and glared at the man he'd called Tulley. "We have any more need of Linquist?"

"Naw. He did real well, Parson."

The bald-headed chieftain looked grateful. "Thanks for your help," he told the ex-railroad employee, then calmly lifted the gun he was holding and shattered Linquist's face with two metal-jacketed rounds.

The reporter felt ill. Quickly, she decided to continue with the farce of an interview to stop herself from vomiting.

"Why don't you tell me who the group is, who runs it, why it exists and its purpose? I've got a newscast to make in less than an hour," she said hurriedly.

Without orders from the head of the group, two of the men dragged the bleeding corpse from the living room and dumped the body in the front hallway.

Ignoring them, Dann babbled about the rights of citizens to bear arms, the invasion of the country by nonwhites, the horror he felt when he saw couples of different races together. He rambled that the decent people in the country—the true Americans—had waited for a Robin Hood to save them from their own corrupt government. And how he had a vision that he was that person.

"What about the bank and armored-car robberies?" the reporter asked.

"If you remember, Robin Hood robbed from the rich to take care of the poor."

Waterman asked another question, "Is that what you intend to do with the money?"

"Eventually, after we win the war."

He started to look bored. "Any other questions?" he asked.

The blonde started to get up from the floor.

"I guess not," she replied. "I better get this tape back to the station so they can get it ready for broadcasting."

Dann reached down and snatched the miniature camera from her hands.

"We'll make sure it gets to your station. Meantime, we want you to be our guest tonight." He grinned at her, some small part of his psychotic personality pushing its way into his voice.

"I'd rather be the one who edits the tape," she said.

She tried again to get to her feet. The leader of The Order shoved her back to the floor.

"You're not going anyplace—except, maybe, to my bedroom upstairs, if you're especially nice to me," he said, ogling her.

Waterman's expression turned to one of horror.

Dann looked at the rest of the gang. "Listen up," he shouted. "Soon's we count the money from tonight's robbery, we'll divvy the money up, pack our things and take a long vacation, just in case someone figures out Linquist was working with us or wonders where this broad is. So start thinking where you'd like to go."

The members of the gang cheered at the news. One of them asked, "Where you planning to go, Parson?"

"Maybe the blonde and me'll head down to Mexico for a while and have some fun," he mused, studying the body of the shocked reporter.

There was a soft movement at the doorway. "Down," he shouted.

As Waterman threw herself against the wooden floor, she heard the clanging of metal from all around her.

A Tec-9 to her right started spitting lead at where the voice had been.

BOLAN HAD ROLLED to the right of the entrance-way, and a fusillade of lead peppered the area where he had been. The soldier was calm as he unleashed a rainstorm of death on the gang members.

Five men were shattered; five men died.

As the racist gang members recovered from the shock of seeing death all around them, the Executioner freed a frag grenade from his belt and pulled the pin.

Counting to five, he pitched the bomb into the center of a group of charging killers. Shrapnel skewered the bodies of the four nearest men. Blood turned the floor around them into a sloppy mess.

Stunned at the sight of brother members dying, the surviving gang members turned their weapons in fury at where Bolan had been standing.

Battle-wise, he had quickly changed locations and emptied the magazine of his Uzi on the closest group of attackers. They looked surprised as high-powered slugs drove through their bodies and pushed them to premature deaths.

Parson Dann had taken cover behind a large easy chair.

Switching weapons, Bolan slid the huge Desert Eagle into his hand and pushed two .44 Magnum loads through the back of the chair.

A muffled cry pierced the room. Dann pulled himself to his feet, staring with disbelief at the Executioner.

"You killed me," he said, as if the possibility had never occurred to him. Then he slid to the floor.

Suddenly desperate without their leader, the remainder of the gang pumped everything they had at Bolan. The soldier spun to his left, freeing another grenade as he did.

The toss was direct—right in the middle of the angry, terrified survivors. The explosion rocked the room, tearing bodies into parts and filling the area with sound and fury.

The soldier carefully checked the fallen soldiers, ready to dispatch at any faking death. None was.

Bolan heard a moan, coming from Parson Dann.

The bald man was having difficulty forming words. "Who told you?"

Bolan lied. "General Lawrence and Senator McCutcheon."

"Bastards," the dying man cursed. "Lawrence had his...men...send us...guns...bullets." Coughing caused the leader of the gang to spit up blood. "Wants to be...President."

His head slumped to one side as death took charge.

The soldier searched for Waterman. Parson Dann had shot the reporter, and Bolan could see blood saturating her white silk blouse.

"It's funny," she gasped as Bolan knelt next

to her. "Biggest story of my life, and I'll never get to see it on television."

Bolan shook his head. He knew she was near death.

"A lot of other people will," he promised.

She began to choke on the blood pouring into her punctured lungs. "Thanks," she whispered, then her head fell to one side as she died.

There was a phone in the hallway, and the Executioner used it to call Brognola.

Quickly, he briefed him on the planned train wreck.

"Consider it handled," Brognola snapped. "What about The Order?"

"Later," Bolan said curtly, then hung up and knelt beside the television reporter. Shoving the videotape in her camcorder into a pocket, he lifted the still form. Blood ran down his blacksuit, but Bolan ignored it.

There was something he had to do before he delivered Wendy Waterman's body and her videotape to her station. Moving to the Jeep, the Executioner set the body of the woman on the back seat, then dug through the canvas carryall to retrieve plastic explosive, along with detonators and timers. He planted the C-4 around the doorways and windows. He knew it was the soldiers of

Phantom Company who dogged his heels. He couldn't be sure exactly when the hit team would get here, so he improvised a trip wire that would automatically set the detonators to trigger the explosives in four minutes.

One-man shooting wars weren't important. What mattered was eliminating the enemy in any way he could.

Bolan drove down the dirt road and pulled the Jeep into a tree-shaded parking place near the main road and turned off the engine.

A variety of military vehicles sped by him, not noticing the Executioner in their rush to get to Parson Dann's place. Leaning on the front fender of the vehicle, the soldier could see car lights being turned off, and the sound of orders being shouted.

He checked the watch on his wrist. Four minutes to go.

Three minutes.

Bolan got behind the wheel and started the engine, glancing at his watch again.

Two minutes.

It was time to get out.

One minute.

The soldier put the Jeep in gear and slowly

drove away from the dirt road. Thirty seconds, twenty, ten.

Suddenly, the sky lit up with the brightness of a holiday fireworks display on the Potomac River. A rush of air pushed out in all directions as light was joined with violent thunder. Under the explosions, Bolan could hear the terrified screams of men as their bodies gave up life.

The Executioner had sent a dozen or more of Phantom Company terrorists on the short journey to hell. It was a fitting tribute to the courageous woman whose body was behind him.

CHAPTER THIRTY-TWO

Sergeant Carter knocked on the door and entered without being invited into the office.

Lawrence looked annoyed. ''What is it, Sergeant?''

''The Phantom team in Maryland, sir. Captain Martin called to say the men were getting restless.''

The general rapped his fingers on his desk. Perhaps now that he was close to being asked to run for office, the Phantom Company had outlived its usefulness.

How to deal with them?

These were professionals, trained in the jungles of Southeast Asia and South America. They had come up against the best, and won. There seemed to be only one solution. Destroy them before they exposed him.

They were gathered at the training site an hour

away from Washington, D.C. He had promised to drive up and discuss his plans for them that afternoon.

This called for a change in strategy, especially with Mack Bolan in the picture.

The wheels in Lawrence's head started turning faster.

There was still Harvey McCutcheon. The senator was a politician, an opportunist. Like Phantom Company, he had outlived his usefulness.

He came up with the ideal solution—take care of the three problems at the same time.

Getting rid of the men in the Phantom Company was relatively easy. Sergeant Carter could arrange for their barracks to be destroyed by plastic explosives.

If the senator had to die—and it was obvious to Lawrence it was time to disassociate himself from the man—he would make sure Mack Bolan was blamed for the crime. Come to think of it, that would also make the President sound like the traitor the general knew he was.

Lawrence lifted the telephone and summoned the sergeant.

"I have something I need done, Sergeant," he said. "I'm sure you have some people who are hungry for work."

THE TWO MEN SAT facing each other in the paneled conference room. The compound known as Stony Man Farm was protected by highly trained people and the latest in the electronic surveillance equipment from human intruders or listening devices.

Located in the Shenandoah Valley, the complex was a community rather than just a base—living quarters, a well-equipped commissary, an armory filled with the latest in military weaponry and a landing pad that could accommodate up to three helicopters, as well as computer equipment that could access the most secure files of domestic federal agencies and foreign counterintelligence agencies were only some of the features of the compound.

A cup of coffee sat before each man, but neither cup had been touched.

"The leak in the White House has been plugged," Brognola reported.

"Lillian Henshaw?"

"Yes. Your reporter, Wendy Waterman picked up an audio tape when she found the woman's body on the sidewalk outside her apartment building. She had tapped into the taping system of the Oval Office."

"Any sense of how the public reacted to her interview with The Order gang?"

"According to polls taken after the broadcast, mostly shock and disbelief."

"Parson Dann and his killers won't be bothering anyone again."

The big Fed nodded. "I saw the police report. Were the men in fatigues all Phantom Company troops?"

"As far as I know. Did you run a check on who ran that operation?"

"Colonel Timmons started it up in Vietnam and probably had a hand in its current deployment. Timmons's body was found yesterday in a D.C. crackhouse. He'd been shot."

"Who did he report to when he was running it?"

"General Mark Lawrence. But don't forget. Lawrence is a living legend to some people."

"Mostly psychopaths," Bolan replied.

He tapped his fingers on the polished hardwood conference table.

"What I need to know is where he could hide a whole company of Green Berets and mercenaries."

"There are a lot of abandoned military bases

in the mountains. I'll check into it," Brognola promised.

Bolan shook his head. "It's hard to believe that one small group—I don't care how powerful it is—could splinter the entire country."

"They didn't. Not every group of nuts that tries to get even with the government is getting backing from outside sources," Brognola agreed. He named several recent brutal bombings that took the lives of hundreds of innocents. Then he added, "But getting rid of those who encourage such actions would go a long way in making these crazies think twice."

The Stony Man Farm chief shuffled through the stack of papers in front of him.

"An undercover agent overheard something. We're not sure that it's legitimate. Lawrence is supposed to be having a secret meeting with Senator McCutcheon."

He handed the typewritten page to the warrior.

"Here's where the meeting is supposed to take place tonight." He hesitated. "If you decide to follow it up, be careful. It could be a setup."

"Only one way to find out," Bolan replied.

THE HOUSE WAS tucked away in a corner of Shady Side, on Chesapeake Bay. Outside, the wooden structure looked like all the others around it, old and ordinary. Inside, the house was set up more like a military headquarters than a home.

A half-dozen military vehicles, all painted olive drab, were parked in front of the building.

Bolan pulled the rental car into a grove of trees and parked. Tiptoeing to the front door of the building, he listened for a moment. There was no sound. He shoved the door open. No one challenged him as he embarked on his search and destroy, going from room to room.

The Executioner quickly made his way through the ground floor, finding it empty. Brognola's informant had to have gotten bad intel. It was as if Phantom Company had been expecting him to appear and had no desire to get into a battle.

Climbing the stairs to the second story, Bolan held the Uzi up and ready, its selector switch set to 3-shot-burst mode.

One by one, he checked the rooms and found each empty.

Moving back down the stairs, Bolan sensed another presence and melted into the shadows.

Two men slowly climbed the stairs.

One of them, a stocky, fatigue-clad soldier gripping a Calico submachine gun in his hands, whispered, "You're sure he came up here?"

"I saw him," the second one vowed.

"Where is he?"

"Maybe he climbed out a window."

"And, I suppose, flew away."

The Executioner stepped in front of the pair.

"No, I'm still here," he replied quietly. "Where's Lawrence?"

One of the gunners tried to fire his submachine gun at Bolan, who drilled three rounds into the surprised terrorist's chest. Slowly, the armed man crumpled to the stairs, then fell backward, tumbling back to the main floor.

Bolan repeated the question.

A hard look crossed the survivor's face.

"Who?"

Bolan aimed low and fired a round into the merc's leg. The terrorist collapsed to one knee, crying in pain.

The soldier repeated the question. "Where's Lawrence?"

"I don't know...."

He saw the Executioner lift the Uzi again.

"No, wait. Please," he whined. "He's not here."

Bolan pointed the Israeli-made weapon at the weeping soldier's legs.

"No, really. He was going to the Phantom

training site." He saw the disbelief in Bolan's face. "No, really."

"Where did they go?"

"The general didn't say."

"Did he say when he was coming back?"

Suddenly, the man on the floor looked frightened. "No," he answered hurriedly.

Bolan became more insistent. "Where did he go?"

The wounded man started to protest. "I don't...." Then he saw the soldier's finger begin to squeeze to the trigger of his weapon. Quickly, he changed his reply.

In a tone of surrender, the wounded man told Bolan where the base was—an abandoned military training site an hour away.

The bullet-ridden merc became unconscious. The Executioner was tempted to kill him to prevent him from possibly warning the general, but killing was a final act when there was no other choice.

Searching the rooms, Bolan found a rope and tied up the man. There was a phone in the room, so he called Brognola and told him where he was and where he was heading.

"Just remember," the Stony Man Farm chief reminded Bolan. "No martyrs."

Without replying, the soldier hung up and went out to where he had parked his car.

As he drove away, the Executioner weighed his options. There weren't many viable ones. Despite the President's admonition about not creating martyrs, Lawrence and his Phantom Company killers had to be stopped.

And there was no better time than now.

CHAPTER THIRTY-THREE

Mark Lawrence was pleased. The tall, stately looking military man smiled at the stout man sitting next to him in the rear of the vinyl-lined luxury-sized car.

Harvey McCutcheon smiled back, wondering why the general had decided to meet in this remote section of Maryland.

"We could have met at my home," he commented.

"Too many ears," Lawrence replied. "Did anybody see you leave?"

"Only the bodyguards."

"What did you tell them?"

"What you suggested. That I was concerned that this mercenary hired by the President was going to try to kill me, so I was getting away for a few days." He paused. "They insisted on going with me, but I made it clear I felt safer if they pretended I was in seclusion in my own home."

"Good." The general looked ahead through the windshield. "We're almost there."

"What was so important that we had to meet in secret?"

"In a moment," the general said. Then he asked, "The campaign to get me nominated. Where does it stand?"

"You're as good as in," the senator replied. "In the eyes of many of the party's leaders, you're exactly what this country needs to establish its greatness again." He took a deep breath. "It's going to take a lot more money than we have to get you elected."

The military hero had looked into the cost of running a campaign. If he was nominated, he knew there would be more than enough money coming in from the groups who believed in eliminating the undesirable elements who were being let into the country.

"That's tomorrow's problem," Lawrence commented. He was relieved. A major hurdle had been jumped. Now it was time to tie up the loose ends. First McCutcheon, then placing the blame for his death at the President's Oval Office.

He leaned forward.

"Sergeant Carter, would you stop the car for a moment?"

The longtime aide to Lawrence understood. He pulled off the road and parked.

McCutcheon looked puzzled. "Is there something wrong?"

Lawrence nodded to the driver.

Gripping a 9 mm Glock 17 pistol in his hand, the noncom turned and carefully fired a trio of rounds into the senator. McCutcheon fell forward, his blood and rent tissue dripping on the seats and floor pads.

"Now there isn't," the general replied.

He leaned forward.

"Sergeant, drive on. The men are waiting for me."

THE EXECUTIONER PULLED the Jeep off the road and parked. Taking out a pair of high-powered binoculars, he studied the supposedly abandoned military camp. A dozen military vehicles were parked near the electrified wire fence that surrounded the compound.

Bolan searched through the canvas bag on the seat next to him and pulled out three bricks of C-4, as well as miniaturized detonators and timers. He'd have to wait until dark to plant the plastic explosive. In the meantime, he'd move as close as he could to the camp.

Getting out of the car, he checked his artillery to make sure each of his weapons had a fresh clip. Stripping off his outer clothes, he exposed the blacksuit he wore on combat missions. A musette bag filled with the explosive components was slung over a shoulder. He hung an Uzi over his other shoulder, and worked his way through the brush toward the military base.

A sudden rush of air knocked the soldier to the ground as a series of explosions ripped through the camp in front of him.

Somebody had gotten here first.

He could hear the screams of men dying inside the barracks buildings. Perhaps a disgruntled former Phantom Company merc had decided to get even.

This wasn't the moment to find out. He would have to search the area and see if General Lawrence had survived the blasts.

THE GENERAL HEARD the explosions and smiled with satisfaction. Phase one of the mission had been accomplished.

He leaned forward. "Congratulations, Sergeant."

The driver nodded.

He estimated that the car was only several hundred yards from the camp. He could take over the driving now. Reaching into his lap, he gripped his Beretta handgun.

"Stop here for a moment," he ordered.

Without question, the noncom pushed down on the brake and put the vehicle in neutral.

"Thank you, Sergeant. For everything," Lawrence said, then held the gun close to the back of Carter's head. Before his aide could complain, the general pulled the trigger twice. The slugs tore out the back of the sergeant's head.

Lawrence got out of the car and opened the front door. He pushed the still bleeding body of the noncom over and, ignoring the gore, got behind the wheel. He put the car in gear and drove slowly toward the camp.

Two men suddenly stepped onto the road in front of his car. Both were in the uniforms of Maryland state troopers.

The general stopped the car. "Something wrong, Officers?"

"Please get out of the car, General," one of them ordered.

Another pair of troopers appeared and shone a light in the back. McCutcheon's body was slumped against the back of the front seats.

One of them gasped. "Good God, that's Senator McCutcheon!"

Lawrence started to explain, then saw the skepticism in the faces of the four officers.

He looked down at the handgun on his lap. For a moment, he thought he could shoot his way out of the ambush, then realized he couldn't.

Before any of the state troopers could stop him, Lawrence shoved the barrel of the Beretta into his mouth and pulled the trigger twice.

The rounds tore through his throat and came out the back of his head. Death came quickly—just as fast as his ambition left him.

A stocky man chewing on an unlit cigar walked up to the car. He glanced inside, then turned away.

"What a waste," he muttered.

BOLAN MADE IT TO WHERE the car was stopped. He had heard the gunfire and grasped the trigger of the Uzi as he let it slide from his shoulder.

Two of the state troopers watched Bolan's approach. Both raised their 9 mm Smith & Wesson pistols, ready to fire at the newcomer's first hostile move.

Brognola put a hand on one of the guns.

"It's okay. He's with me."

The troopers lowered their weapons, still staring suspiciously at the Executioner.

"What happened?" Bolan asked.

Brognola told him.

The soldier shook his head, then lowered his voice.

"If he hadn't done it, I was ready to deal with the situation."

"I know."

"At least there are no martyrs."

"Good work, Striker."

Bolan thought of the hundreds of groups still free to terrorize the country. "It's only beginning. There's a whole world of fear and hate waiting to tear this country apart. I've still got a long way to go before it's finished."

His voice filled with sadness, Brognola replied, "I know. But it had to start somewhere. Let me know when you want to take on some of the others."

"Later," he said, then turned and walked back to where he had left the Jeep.

He needed time out to take care of his wounds and his feelings about those who had already died in the war to save the country from itself.

Gold Eagle brings you high-tech action
and mystic adventure!

THE Destroyer™

#119 Fade to Black
Created by
MURPHY
and SAPIR

Art begins to imitate life in Tinsel Town as real-life events are mir-
rored in small independent films...and the U.S. President's life is
placed in jeopardy.

Available in April 2000 at your favorite retail outlet.

Shadow THE EXECUTIONER®
as he battles evil for 352 pages of heart-stopping action!

SuperBolan®

#61452	DAY OF THE VULTURE	$5.50 U.S.	☐
		$6.50 CAN.	☐
#61453	FLAMES OF WRATH	$5.50 U.S.	☐
		$6.50 CAN.	☐
#61454	HIGH AGGRESSION	$5.50 U.S.	☐
		$6.50 CAN.	☐
#61455	CODE OF BUSHIDO	$5.50 U.S.	☐
		$6.50 CAN.	☐
#61456	TERROR SPIN	$5.50 U.S.	☐
		$6.50 CAN.	☐

(limited quantities available on certain titles)

TOTAL AMOUNT	$
POSTAGE & HANDLING	$
($1.00 for one book, 50¢ for each additional)	
APPLICABLE TAXES*	$ _____
TOTAL PAYABLE	$ _____
(check or money order—please do not send cash)	

To order, complete this form and send it, along with a check or money order for the total above, payable to Gold Eagle Books, to: **In the U.S.:** 3010 Walden Avenue, P.O. Box 9077, Buffalo, NY 14269-9077; **In Canada:** P.O. Box 636, Fort Erie, Ontario, L2A 5X3.

Name: _____

Address: _____ City: _____

State/Prov.: _____ Zip/Postal Code: _____

*New York residents remit applicable sales taxes.
 Canadian residents remit applicable GST and provincial taxes.

GSBBACK1